14/6/89   4.95

THE HEART

Fay Weldon was born and brought up in New Zealand, and went to St Andrew's University, Scotland, where she graduated in Economics and Psychology. After a decade of odd jobs and hard times, she started writing and now, though primarily a novelist (*Praxis*, *Puffball* and *Life and Loves of a She-Devil* amongst them) she also writes short stories, radio dramas, and is a prolific stage and screen writer.

The Heart of the Country

FAY WELDON

ARROW BOOKS

Arrow Books Limited
62-65 Chandos Place, London WC2N 4NW

An imprint of Century Hutchinson Ltd

London Melbourne Sydney Auckland
Johannesburg and agencies throughout
the world

First published in Great Britain by Hutchinson 1987
Arrow edition 1987

Reprinted 1987

Printed and bound in Great Britain by
Anchor Brendon Ltd, Tiptree, Essex

ISBN 0 09 953340 5

The Wages of Sin

Oh, the wages of sin!

Natalie Harris sinned, and her husband Harry left for work one fine morning and didn't come back.

The morning was fine only temporarily. You know what those mornings are, just before the rain sets in? Bright and glittery around the edges; altogether too bright for safety, with a pale blue sky arching much too high above, and beyond the arch heaven knows what, God or the Devil. And before you know it black clouds begin to edge up all around the horizon, like muddy water welling from a blocked drain, and close the sky over with cloud, drizzle and depression, and your quivering glimpse of eternity, good or bad, is gone. There's just the bus to catch or the washing up to get on with. Just such a too bright morning it was, when Harry Harris left for work and didn't return, leaving Natalie Harris well and truly in the shit, if you'll excuse me.

But well and truly there she was, floundering in the excreta (if the word seems less offensive) the human race spits out behind it as it gallops on in search of profit and diversion. Left holding the baby, what's more – that is to say the two Harris children, Ben and Alice: not everyone's cup of tea, these two less than innocent mites, and certainly not mine, but Natalie loved them, as mothers love their children, blindly.

It was a Thursday morning. It seemed much like any other. Natalie got up at 7.10. The radio alarm switched itself on: music and chat came through loud and clear. The Harris' nice new bungalow, complete with dream kitchen, picture windows and parquet floors, lay in the shadow of the Mendip Mast, that vital, quivery, silver wand which reaches up into the sky, erected by man on the highest spot available, in other words as near as can be to the ethereal god of Telecommunications. And Dunbarton, the Harris' home, on the outskirts of Eddon Gurney, just eight miles from the Mast and halfway between Wells and Glastonbury, had the full benefit of it.

Harry still lay asleep in the twin bed. He'd been home late the night before. Natalie took twenty minutes washing, dressing, plucking, preening. (The rest of us pull on a pair of jeans and yesterday's sweater: not Natalie.) She let Jax the Alsatian out and Tweeny her little grey cat in. (Cats should be kept in at night: it is brutal to do otherwise, but Natalie didn't know this. How ignorant she was at this stage in her life!) At 7.35 she woke Ben and Alice. They had separate rooms. Alice kept hers tidy and Ben his untidy. At 7.40 she woke Harry and offered him a choice of shirts. (She ironed on Sunday and Wednesday evenings, watching television.) But Harry took his best white silk slimline from the very back of the cupboard and wore that. Natalie was glad when Harry had a shirt, any shirt, on his back. She did not like the texture of his skin. It seemed to her to be too white, too soft, too spotty. They'd been living in the Pipeline Road, Banjul and there at least, under the African sun, his skin had been brown and tougher and younger.

At 8.35 Harry drove off in his Cortina; Natalie and the children stood in the front porch and waved goodbye. Even Jax the dog sat and stared.

'Don't be late tonight!' said Natalie. 'Remember we have people to dinner.'

'I'll be back at six-thirty,' he said, 'On the dot!' and

they kissed each other and Harry drove off. How anyone watching would have admired and envied that particular domestic tableau, under the glittery sun.

Mind you, I'm not surprised the Harris household was in trouble. It lived in yet another shadow, being equidistant from the Mendip Mast and Glastonbury Tor. This latter is the solid, ancient hummocky hill which dominates the flat lands in the Somerset Southwest, and from some angles looks like a lady's breast. It's tipped by a crumbling tower, which those who're determined claim looks like that breast's erect nipple. So you could say if you are determined – and many who live round here are – that the Mast was male and the Tor was female: certainly the Mast is modern and the Tor ancient. The Tor transmits as well, if you ask me, though rather fitfully: probably alpha waves from King Arthur's sleeping brain. The great king is buried in the grounds of Glastonbury Abbey, at the foot of the Tor; not dead, they say, but sleeping, to wake in the hour of England's need. And this is it, if you ask me. So the alpha waves have been hotting up lately, and he's stirring all right, and what with the Tor transmitting its mystic messages of oneness, allness, wholeness, and so forth, and the Mast streaming out Dallas and Robin Day, it's not surprising the Harris household quivered and shook and broke into little bits. Well, that's about the only excuse I can think of for Harry Harris, who wasn't a bad guy, really. Just panicky about his life and his business, which was failing.

Some said, unkindly, when they heard Harry Harris hadn't come home but had run off with Miss Eddon Gurney 1978, she with the blonde cloud of hair and the thin lips, how did his wife *know* he hadn't come home? I mean, could she *tell?* And it was true that this ordinary

3

businessman in his Ford Cortina, with his ordinary hair-cut, suit and tie, this apparently conventional business-man, so conventionally these days into computers, did seem to melt into the background of the village and be what we expect of our neighbours, rather than our-selves – that is to say, to be ordinary, anonymous and under control. He did listen a great deal to Radio 2, however, a station which beams out olden goldies – or is it golden oldies? – and feeds the nostalgic and romantic imagination, daily reviving memories of long lost youth. This should perhaps have warned Natalie her husband was in love. In love. Ah!

In love with Miss Eddon Gurney 1978. The carnival queen. His secretary. Even village beauties must work, these days.

Picture Natalie. Round face, blonde-haired, pretty as a girl in an early Charlie Chaplin movie, with that same blank look of sexy idiocy on her face. It was as if she was born to go round with subtitles: *Help me, save me. Poor little me.* It was how she had been brought up to look: not her fault. And, as it turned out, when faced by disaster she was in fact competent enough. In fact, by the end of the story – or as much of it as I'm in a position to tell – Natalie was looking less like a heroine and more like a call girl, but that's life, isn't it? Carry on a decade or two, or three, and I daresay she'll look like a little old lady. A little old lady or a little old man, that's where all our futures lie. What does it matter? It's what happens on the way that counts.

And listen, Harry Harris not coming home that evening was at least something *happening*, wasn't it! If he had come home, life would have gone on as per usual for ever, Natalie dream walking, Harry sleep-walking, and that would have been even worse than disaster for both of them. Natalie was lucky. It's not

4

everyone's good fortune to have things *occur* in their lives, just like that, out of the blue. No, usually if you want things to change you have to make them change, and most of us don't want the responsibility. So we do nothing and drift on in unsatisfactory situations, waiting for magic, which doesn't happen.

The saving disaster happens in our heads, of course. Don't tell me you've never imagined your nearest and dearest dead or swallowed up or gone: swum out to sea and not come back, the house burnt down or the Bomb fallen. And imagining it is wanting it. Of course, if it really happened – well, pray God or the Devil it hasn't, it won't – if it does your guilt won't make it easier to bear. That's what I mean by the wages of sin.

Whose sin? Harry's? Natalie's? Natalie, let it be said, was having an affair with a certain Arthur Wandle, an antique dealer in the Somerset market town of Eddon Gurney. Arthur Wandle had a well-situated and prosperous shop which nestled just at the foot of Gurney Castle, and was much frequented in the summer by tourists. In the winter business was quieter, and Arthur used to like to spend Tuesdays and Thursdays from November through to March, when his wife Jane was helping out at the Junior School, with whoever it was it happened to be. This year it was Natalie.

Natalie dreamed and sleepwalked into the room behind the antique shop and took off her clothes and let herself be fucked – if you'll excuse my language. Look, everyone knows the word, even the children; and fuck me, and I'll be fucked, and all fucked up – and she was, you see, Natalie was. I use the word advisedly. What do you want me to say? Made love to? She wasn't. Okay, okay, intercourse took place between her and Arthur and very nice too. I'm just making the point it wasn't love: love would have been far more

5

dangerous. Pow! Wham! Into the lives of the settled love comes like a great cosmic screwdriver lifting off the lid of a pot of paint: and before you know it the lid's left off, the paint's skinned over, and no use to anyone. There's a metaphor for you! Miss Eddon Gurney prised off the top of Harry's paint pot all right: Arthur didn't Natalie's. Natalie's paint just stayed there undisturbed, rich, thick and glorious.

Anyway, when Harry Harris didn't come home Natalie's first thought was, oh, this is all my fault. I have betrayed my husband. Another man has entered in where no other man has any right to be. It's all my fault and I am being punished. But of course it wasn't like that at all. Harry Harris had run off with Miss Eddon Gurney, knowing nothing at all about Natalie's Tuesdays and Thursdays behind the antique shop in Eddon Gurney. And if he had known, I really don't think he would have cared.

Now I don't want you to lose sympathy with either Harry or Natalie, especially Natalie (if only because Harry Harris has already vanished – well, as much as the father of a woman's children can ever be said to vanish from her life) because up till then they both of them had been trying to do the right thing, be serious and responsible people. It's just life gets so *boring*, doesn't it? And there was a kind of hole where Natalie's heart was supposed to be, the kind that nature abhors, and she would have loved Arthur if only she could, and thus sanctified the relationship. Oh, excuses, excuses! Natalie did wrong. Forgive her. She meets her comeuppance the day our story begins. Let that be enough for you.

Harry Harris ran off leaving his wife living in a dream bungalow mortgaged up to the hilt and beyond, no money in the bank and school fees owing. He left her with no job, unqualified and untrained, and with no experience other than as a businessman's wife and mother of two extremely self-centred children, aged eleven and twelve. Would you wish to be in such a position? And would you not think that any woman married to a man capable of doing such a thing would not perhaps be having an affair with someone *nicer* than her husband? Who was *not* capable of so doing? She was – which meant that Arthur, being nicer, had no intention of deserting or abandoning his wife and running off with Natalie when she became, as it were, free. In other words, she just couldn't win.

But there you are. Women who live by the good will of men have no control over their lives, and that's the truth of it.

'What do you mean?' Natalie asked Hilary, the receptionist of Harrix, Harry Harris' firm. 'What do you mean he's not in? He left for work early so he'd be back early. We have important people coming for dinner.'

'I think I'd better come round, Mrs Harris,' said Hilary, thinking she should break the news gently, face to face. On account of how she didn't think Mr Harris was going to be there for dinner, no matter how many important people had been asked. And thus she did break the news, and little thanks she got for it.

But we're running ahead of ourselves.

Natalie had rung Harry at the office because all of a sudden she was worried. She was worried because when she drove the children to school that morning the school office had called her in and told her school fees for two terms were outstanding. The school secretary had actually come out to the car when she was dropping Ben and Alice off and asked her to step inside for just a minute –

'If you don't mind, Mrs Harris.' Mrs Harris did mind.

Wouldn't you mind? Mrs Harris wasn't so different from anyone else – neurotic about money. She never added up her cheque stubs and hated going into the bank for fear of what she would find out. And if the phone rang behind the counter when she was there, she jumped, imagining it was her financial misdeeds catching up with her, there and then. Mrs Harris nevertheless smiled politely, listened to the school secretary's tale of loss and woe, shook her head in apparent sympathy and said –

'My husband's changing secretaries: I expect that's it. Files have got muddled, or something. I'll ask him to see to it at once. I'm so sorry you've been inconvenienced.'

And later Pauline from the delicatessen rode up on her old-fashioned bicycle with the week's order, and pointed out that the Harris' account now topped the hundred-pound mark and could she take steps to pay?

'Good heavens, my husband must have overlooked it,' Natalie said. 'I'll make sure it's seen to, Pauline.' By this time Natalie was really put out. Harry, she felt, ought to stand between her and these embarrassments.

But it wasn't until Natalie realized that Harry hadn't even left the usual five pound note to pay Flora the cleaner that she decided to call him at his office.

Pow! Wham! Oh, the wages of sin.

Only five pounds for four hours' work! It wasn't much. But Harry argued that Flora was only eighteen, was an indifferent cleaner – albeit the best that could be found – and that if she was paid more the market would be spoiled for other employers.

How much do you pay your cleaner? If you have one? Or how much are you paid, if you go out cleaning yourself? I tell you, it's not enough. It can never be enough. For his unkindness, for his blindness, Harry

Harris deserves to be unhappy with Miss Eddon Gurney 1978, though I don't suppose he will be. Natalie, consenting to the paying of Flora the sum of one pound twenty-five pence an hour, was an accessory after the fact, an accomplice, but deserved even worse inasmuch as Flora is, politically and in the feminist sense, her sister, her little helpless sister, living as Flora did in a caravan on the site of the council garbage tip, there where the crows wheel and fly. Flora lived with Bernard, who was unemployed. (Unemployment amongst the rural under 25's is reckoned, currently, at around 60 per cent.) Flora's heels were downtrodden: it was bad for her young legs; they bowed outward from the knee. Her diet was bad, too, and her clothes were too thin in cold weather. Amazing, really, how beautiful she managed to be, beneath a halo of black, yellow and green greasy-spiked hair, solid with hair gel and spray: like an angel ascending, not even falling. Even Harry had noticed how lovely she was – but not enough not to cheat her: one pound twenty-five pence the hour for washing the flecks of hair from the basin after Harry had shaved; for picking up the Harris children's toys; for wiping the grease from where it accumulated behind the mixer taps of the kitchen sink – you know, that rather sexy dip at the start of the stem?

The wages of sin! Harry sinned; Natalie paid. So did Flora.

Now the section of countryside between the Mendip Mast and Glastonbury Tor is extremely pretty – though, as I say, troubled by the mystic forces I speak of. There are winding country lanes and sudden hills, and sheep graze and cottages nestle and villages drowse, even though round every other bend there's a concrete bunker, a tin barn, a quarry and an intensive pig breeding unit. The fact is, the heart of the country's rotten: I really believe it is. No wonder Harry sinned. How can a people be better than its rulers? If the rulers put profit and practicality first, how can the people be expected to do better? Take Harry: now the way out of Harry's financial difficulties was flight. The most practical person to fly with was not his wife, but Miss Eddon Gurney, who was single, childless and unafraid. Of course he went. It was profitable and practical to do so. Wouldn't you, in his shoes? No? Look at it this way. Harry and Natalie slept together, ate together, had children together; but that was the limit of their intimacy. They exchanged information, not feelings or ideas.

'I've booked the car in for a service, darling,' she'd say, over breakfast.

'Thank you, darling,' he'd say, and off he'd go to work. Anyone can talk like that. Why Natalie rather than another? Why stay?

They were helpful and polite to each other, and never quarrelled. Why bother? They might even have believed they were happy together, had Harry not discovered himself really quite interested in what Marion Hopfoot, voted carnival queen in 1978, had to say, which was that she was in love with him, and Natalie not discovered herself in Arthur's arms, rolling off the Victorian chaise longue on to the rather nice rag rug before the little coal fire in the register grate, intertwined and even more wonderfully energetic on the floor than the sofa. Ah, conversation. Oh, love. Ah, sex. Oh, again, consequences!

The consequence was:

'I'd better come round,' Hilary, Harry's receptionist, said, and so she did. She had a pale face and a domed forehead and too large pop eyes, and a practical manner. Many a man would follow her to the ends of the earth, had she chosen to go. She knew exactly what to do, and when and how, and would never have dreamed of going. A wonderful gift! She had beautiful breasts too – white energetic domes, cherry-tipped, and these gave her confidence in the world – but Hilary hardly enters the story, she or her chest. She is merely the bearer of bad news, standing in Natalie's dream kitchen – oak-veneered cupboards, brass fittings, wall oven and ceramic hob, and a black-and-white tiled floor recently rather badly washed by Flora. Hilary's waist was tightly belted, the better to show off her figure, and her frog eyes were moist with pity and indignation mixed.

The wages of sin!

'The staff haven't been paid for two weeks,' said Miss Hilary Frog. 'Mr Harris said it was just a cash-flow problem but most of us in computers know where that kind of thing leads. It's a high risk business, isn't it? If you haven't got the capital, that is – and Mr Harris hadn't. My boyfriend's father is a friend of the bank manager and he told us Harrix was seriously under-funded. Then, when he didn't turn up today, and Marion neither – '

'Marion?' Natalie had never heard her name before. Truly. It's most often a bolt from the blue which strikes down a good wife and mother, especially when she's economically dependent. Don't let me frighten you – unless it's into getting a training and a job. You know what the statistics for these things are? You know how many marriages end in divorce? One in three. And a recent survey shows that a woman's standard of living falls on average by 42 per cent after divorce, and a man's actually *rises* . . . Enough!

'Marion?'

'Marion Hopfoot,' said Hilary. 'She's his secretary.

He's been seeing a lot of her. That is to say, not just in office hours, which would be natural, but after hours as well. Well, you must have known. Oh. No? Oh dear! But Marion told us it was all okay, you knew all about it and didn't mind. And one of the fellers told me you and that antique dealer up by the Castle – but that's none of my business. Well, every marriage is different, isn't it?'

'I suppose it is,' said Natalie.

'But this morning, when Mr Harris didn't turn up, and Marion didn't either, we got to wondering and one of the technicians called her home and Marion's mother answered. She said Marion had left a note saying she was running off to Spain with Harry Harris. And it must be true because she'd taken her passport. So everyone reckoned that was that. They called the police because of the unpaid wages.'

'Police?' said Natalie.

'And then *you* rang, Mrs Harris. So I reckon that's that. Sixteen people out of a job, if you don't count Marion Hopfoot.'

Natalie sat on the kitchen table, swinging her left leg idly and thinking of Hilary's frog eyes and that Hilary's bosom was over the top but unable to take in all that much of what Hilary actually said. She felt like a cobra which has swallowed a donkey and finds it too large to digest and too awkward to spit out. She couldn't somehow make sense of anything.

'There's hardly any petrol in the car,' she observed.

'So?' inquired Hilary. Hilary was having to do without two weeks' wages and none at all in lieu of notice, and felt that Natalie was not the only one with troubles. 'And I've got no money and Harry doesn't believe in credit cards – not for me, anyhow – though he's got a gold American Express. There's enough

12

petrol for this afternoon, I expect, but how am I going to get the children to school tomorrow morning?'

How indeed? Of such boring problems are tragedies made. Natalie, the perfect mother, the tidy dresser, she who turned up at school every morning with her tights unladdered and her face properly made up and a pretty little scarf round her neck, bringing out the colour of her somewhat blank blue eyes – I tell you, little Mrs Tippy-toes was sleepwalking, poor thing, and had been for 15 years or so, ever since she married Harry Harris. Only now she suddenly perceived she might not be able to get to the school gates *at all*. And this, it suddenly came to her, might well be the wages of sin. The first thing a woman who suffers misfortune feels is *guilty*. *My fault*, she is convinced. Something I did wrong. She may well be right.

And Natalie had a great deal to be guilty about, when you come to think of it. Consider her sins that very day.

The sin of lust: as envisaged with Arthur. She was looking forward to it. It's as bad to contemplate it as to do it.

The sin of envy: envying Flora's looks, and making her dust an already dusted sideboard. Mahogany – veneered, but sealed with polyurethane and very, very shiny.

The sin of pride: despising Hilary because she had a too-large bosom (by Natalie's standards) and frog eyes.

The sin of sloth: not bothering to know what was going on in Harry's life, heart and bank account; asking Pauline to deliver her groceries, instead of collecting them herself. Pauline was older than Natalie and had a harder life.

The sin of gluttony: buying smoked salmon for dinner. Scottish, not Canadian. Twice the price, and pity the poor fish! Followed up by chicken. Horrid white stringy stuff, from a mangy bird which lived and died in a box.

The sin of avarice: underpaying Flora on Harry's instructions. The less she paid Flora, the more pairs of shoes Natalie could buy. Natalie loved shoes: they were her extravagance. She owned eighteen pairs, and fifteen of these had high heels, so when the hard times came she had only three for getting about in, and two of those were sandals.

And the special sin of splashing the poor.

You may not know about this one: it's a modern sin. It's what happens, say, on the School Run. If you're driving the children to school on a rainy day and you pass too close to the mothers and children who don't have cars, who have to walk, and you drench them with the mud of your passing. We are here in this world to be scavengers: to pick up the dregs and dust of creation and save what's possible and render it back to the Almighty, not to hang about carelessly, adding to the mud, the trouble and confusion. We are meant to be salvagers, not wreckers.

Natalie had sinned badly that morning, taking her children to school (private, of course), driving too close to Sonia, an unsupported mother, who, with Edwina (4), Bess (5) and Teresa (6) filed along the busy road in the rain, as close in to the prickly hedge as they could, for fear of sudden death on their way to a school (not private, of course) which all three children hated, but which the law obliged them to attend. Natalie simply didn't see them: she didn't even notice they were there.

Alice, Natalie's little girl, noticed. Alice said, 'It's raining. Why don't we give them a lift?'

Ben said: 'You're so stupid, Alice. We don't give lifts to people like that.'

14

But Natalie just said, peering through a misty wind-screen, which neither wipers nor demister at full blast would clear: 'Do be quiet, children,' without actually hearing a word they were saying. In her defence it was a nasty morning for driving, but that is not the kind of excuse the Prime Mover likes to hear. He, after all, sends the rain. He worked in his mysterious way, and Sonia helped. She looked after the retreating five-door Volvo Estate. (Of course it was a Volvo. What else?) Jax the Alsatian, the Harris' dog, looked back at Sonia and grinned. Even the dogs of the rich live better than do the new poor. The dogs ride; the poor walk, or go by bus. There are very few buses anymore in the countryside. The rich don't take them. That means buses don't, on the whole, make profits. So they have to be subsidized. But who's going to subsidize them? The rich, who don't need them or use them? Ho, ho!

'God rot her,' said Sonia aloud. 'Rich bitch!' Sonia had been born a nice round pleasant thing. Her life and times had turned her sour, so now she could deliver a curse or two, effectively. God heard. God sent his punishment on Natalie. Or was it the Devil? He forgave her other sins, but got her for this one. Natalie committed the sin of carelessly splashing Sonia. Sonia cursed her. Misfortune fell on Natalie. Cause and effect? Surely not. Let's just say coincidence, and remind ourselves that the trouble at Harrix and in the Harris household long predated this particular event. Except of course God may send his punishments retro-spectively. We may all of us be being punished *now* for sins we are about to commit. Time may not be as linear as we suppose.

'What have I done?' asked Natalie, pretty white sinful hand, used to exploring Arthur's chest hairs, to her mouth. She addressed the universe as much as Hilary.

15

Well, as I say, the wages of sin! There's no telling. The day Natalie Harris splashed Sonia with mud was the day Harry Harris left for work in the morning and did not return home, ever. Some sins are obviously worse than others.

The Pleasures of Adultery

Pleasure I said, pleasure I meant. Adulterate means to spoil, to pollute. It also contains the sense of dilution by poison. It's dropping a spot of cochineal into the white icing sugar and water mix and watching the colour spread – great streaks of vile red circling out with the first stir from that single central drop, gradually easing and diluting as you work into bland universal pink. So what (to change the metaphor, while keeping it domestic) if it's like a blind tumbling right off its roller when you tug, bringing down with it in a cloud of dust every concept of honour, dignity, integrity, fidelity or trust you ever had! So what if you can't raise the blind, and have to stay in the dark for ever! It's worth it. That's what I think.

Rot you, I said to Natalie. Rich bitch! Rot you. I, Sonia, cursed her. And her world fell down, clatter, clatter, clatter. Good!

There, I have blown my cover. The 'I' who speaks to you is Sonia. In my quest for sanity and self-improvement I do my docile best, as instructed by my psychiatrist, to objectivize myself and see myself as others see me – that is to say in the third person – when and as I enter into Natalie's story. In Chapter One I reckon I just about succeeded. But 'The Pleasures of Adultery' have clearly been too much for me: in my excitement I have revealed all. Well, let's get on. The tale is about Natalie, not me. A writer's exercise in ego reduction! I do apologize for the 'good!' at the end of

17

the previous paragraph. One should wish no one harm. But it's what I felt, so there it stays, unedited.

The first thing Natalie did after Hilary left in dudgeon was go round and see Arthur. It was her afternoon for visiting, anyway. Thursday. Arthur's wife Jane went round to one of the local schools to 'hear reading' every Tuesday and Thursday afternoon between 2 and 3.30. Not much time, you might think, for Natalie and Arthur to do what they liked to do and still have time for a little talk about this and that, and a courtship ritual or so. A murmur in the other's ear about life, love, happiness, remorse, the state of their own and the other's soul. That, if you ask me, is the main pleasure of adultery. Not the sex, but the painful, pleasurable examination of the psyche, that acknowledgement of sin which accompanies the sex. Marriage declines into what's for dinner? Who's going to pay this month's mortgage? Is buggery okay for you? When all we really want to think about is God and eternity. Guilt brings us nearer to God. Natalie, Mrs Tippy-toes, trit-trotting on her little high heels into Arthur's shop, (she wore absurd shoes for someone living in the country: as if her natural habitat was Bond Street) was doing her best to get nearer to God.

You believe that? You'll believe anything.

Arthur specialized in old English oak and oriental antiquities: a peculiar mixture but one which worked well enough in Eddon Gurney. His wife Jane dusted and cleaned around, and when Arthur was out kept shop. Sometimes, when she was really angry and upset by Arthur, she would drop and break something and there'd be a few hundred pounds down the drain. Arthur looked on it as a kind of tax he had to pay to the God of Marriage. He fucked, she dropped. It was inevitable. He sighed but did not scold. It kept the balance between them. Jane would clean the little back room behind the shop; smooth the covers on the chaise longue, shake out the pillows, hoover and straighten the rag rug, polish the register grate in which, in winter, Arthur liked to keep a coal fire going. It was in this room that Arthur did his books and added up his VAT, and where he retired when customers came in he couldn't stand the look of. Jane had a pretty good idea this was where he brought his women, but she cleaned and dusted it all the same.

Jane and Arthur lived above the shop. They had an excellent view of the stone walls of Gurney Castle. Jane was a little, pretty, anxious woman: she jumped if anything startled her. She was too thin: she looked as if a harsh word would make her snap in the middle. Arthur was tall, big, broad, serene, handsome. A villain: of course he was a villain: but his chest was large enough for at least two or three troubled women to lay their heads upon – it seemed wasted otherwise. What could Jane do? She couldn't not go out, ever, for fear of what Arthur would do in her absence. She did try for many years to leave the house unexpectedly, to keep altering her shopping-visiting routine, as those who live in danger of kidnapping do, but a pattern kept emerging even in her unpredictability. Or else it was that Arthur could read her mind? She'd say on a Wednesday evening she was going to stay overnight with her mother who needed cheering up. On Thursday lunchtime she'd come back and there was just that *feel* in Arthur's back room: a butterfly hair clip under the rag rug: once a pair of bikini pants stuffed in a Venetian punch bowl –

'They must have been there when I bought it – over-priced anyway' – was all Arthur said.

So really she gave up. She took up the Tuesday and

Thursday work at the school – unpaid of course, but someone has to hear the beginners, and the teacher sure as hell doesn't have the time, what with thirty or so little faces staring up in every class – and Jane and Arthur had no children of their own, and Jane loved children, loved them – and took some comfort from the fact that Arthur always made love to her on Tuesday and Thursday nights. Sex begets more sex. Made love, I said, not fucked. Arthur loved his wife. Otherwise he might not have bothered to torment her so and she'd have been an altogether plumper and younger-looking woman, who warmed her hands by the fire and laid her head on Arthur's chest. Jane wondered who it was who visited. She had thought it might be Natalie Harris but when Natalie asked her and Arthur to dinner at Dunbarton, out of the blue, she decided it couldn't be. If she was Arthur's secret woman she wouldn't have the nerve.

Wouldn't she just!

Anyway, that Thursday afternoon Natalie went into Arthur's shop in quite a state. Now Natalie was very much alone in the world. Both her parents were dead. Her father had been in the air force: he'd been forty when she was born, her mother thirty-five. The family had moved from one air-force base to another throughout the world. Her father had died of bone cancer: nothing to do, the authorities swore, with the fact that he was on the maintenance side of the air-force business, and his speciality the nuclear missile-carrying capacity of conventional aircraft. And God knows what his fingers had dabbled in since 1946, or what warning bells and flashing red lights he had ignored in the pursuance of his duty.

Be that as it may, he was dead by fifty-five and his wife died of throat cancer fairly soon after. Natalie seemed healthy enough; just parentless and friendless. She'd been to twelve schools throughout her childhood, and childhood friends just hadn't had a chance to stick. She was halfway through secretarial college when she was sent for work experience to temp at Harrix, then assembling not home computers but digital watches, in East London. Harry took her out a few times and then proposed, and she accepted. It had not even been a good secretarial college. Natalie could arrange flowers and man the front office, but she couldn't shorthand-type. Or was it wouldn't? She was bright as a button, pretty as a picture and just plain stunned: hit hard on the head by loss and loneliness. If now, unloved by Harry, she laid her head on Arthur's chest, who was to blame her? Not me: all I blame her for is splashing me on the way to school that morning. That I do find hard to forgive. Even orphans should take a look at the world outside and notice what's going on.

'I suppose *you* can't pay my wages?' Hilary had asked that Thursday morning when the wages of sin announced their intention of getting paid, and Natalie had shaken her head. How? Hilary had looked round the dream kitchen, and slid her foot over the parquet floor, and raised her eyebrows, just a little.

'It's not just your bad news,' observed Hilary. 'It's all our bad news. Sixteen of us working up there at Harrix, not counting Marion Hopfoot, who never does a stroke anyway, and no wages for two weeks. Some of the men with mortgages! And if this job goes where are any of us going to find another one? You know what it's like round here.'

Natalie pondered.

Natalie said, presently, 'The last thing Harry said to me this morning was that he'd see me at six-thirty. So

21

I'm just going to carry on as usual, and at six-thirty this evening he'll turn up, and explain everything.'

'You are a fool!' Hilary had banged on a kitchen cupboard as she spoke and the cups and plates inside trembled. 'Of course he's not coming back. The petty cash is empty. I rang the bank: he went round to collect the wages all right, first thing, and he had to argue and fight for them, from what I hear; then he just disappeared. He's gone. Done a bunk.'

'There's no need to get so excited,' said Natalie. 'If the bank's proving so difficult, he's probably changed to another. My husband is always changing banks. In fact I expect that's where he's gone. To Bath, or Bristol. He'll be back!'

'You're mad!' said Hilary, banging away, bosom bouncing.

'We had a half-a-million-pound order coming in, and he borrowed on the strength of it, and then the order didn't come through. No bank's going to look at him after that. Mrs Harris, I repeat, your husband has *done a bunk.*'

'Um,' said Natalie politely, and Hilary had left, without so much as being offered a cup of anything. Natalie had run out of instant coffee. Not surprising. These days it costs one pound ninety-five pence the jar. Monstrous! How hard it is to keep the mind off minor irritations even when major disasters threaten. Natalie bathed, changed into her best slip and knickers, and walked all the way up to Arthur's to save petrol. But somehow not even the walk relaxed her.

'Nat-Nat,' said Arthur, drawing the unusually stiff-limbed but silkily clad Natalie into his back room. 'It's been a long long time since Tuesday.' His suit was agreeably warm, and smelt of Antiquax, the best polish available for real wood. Natalie laid her head briefly

22

upon his chest, in a kind of obeisance to past pleasures. But then, surprising herself as much as him, she drew back and away.

'I can't,' she said.

'Time of the month?' he asked. 'I don't mind.' He didn't either, unlike Harry, whom menstruation made nervous.

'It's not that,' she said. 'Just perhaps we shouldn't go on doing this.'

'Is it having Jane and me coming to dinner tonight? Is that the matter?' he asked. 'You mustn't worry. I won't give you away.'

'That's nothing to do with it,' said Natalie. And it wasn't, though it should have been. How many meals have *you* taken, do you think, when there's been something going on between your partner and A. N. Other that you haven't known about? Don't to this day? What winkings, glimmerings and nudgings? Doesn't bear thinking about. Could quite put you off your food.

'What, then? Hubby hot on the trail?' He was concerned. He had kind, thoughtful eyes, for a villain. He made love beautifully, gently, commandingly, unerringly and altogether without doubt, as it were, as to his capacity for his pleasure or his partner's – though always, of course, in something of a hurry in case his wife came back.

'I don't think so,' said Natalie, but she did wonder. Perhaps Harry had found out, taken offence, taken off. What then? But she couldn't admit it; nor could she understand the phenomenon of her sexual reluctance. As well take off her clothes now for Arthur as take them off in Wells Cathedral in the middle of Sunday Service! She was afflicted, in fact, by superstitious dread. If she put another foot wrong the ice might crack; she'd go through, go under, drown. It might indeed be true that Harry was no more, that six-thirty would come and go and he not appear: not a trace of him left behind – except the children, that is. She must reassemble herself in her own head as an ordinary, faithful wife to which untoward events did not occur. Then surely everything would be all right. Oh yes, wife and mother Natalie, neat and clean, looking out of the mirror back at her complacent self. Smile for the camera, Natalie! Good Natalie! Keep your fingers crossed, not to mention your legs!

You wonder how I know all this? What goes on in one woman's head goes pretty much on in another's, or else why can doctors (male) ask their ritual questions about hormonal levels – viz: Do you feel murderous *before* your period or after your period, madam? – and feel safe in prescribing dangerous drugs according to your answer?

We are all of us part of one bleeding body, if you ask me.

So Natalie went home from Arthur's with her hair unruffled and her skirt unlifted, leaving Arthur puzzled, but at least able to get on with filling in his VAT forms. And as it happened Jane came back from school almost as soon as she'd arrived, the teachers having called a one-day strike in the furtherance of a pay claim, and ventured to surprise her husband in the back room. But she found him just sitting there, all innocence.

Whew!

'I'm mad,' Jane told herself. 'Paranoid. I need treatment. Why do I have these neurotic fantasies that my husband's being unfaithful to me? It must be something to do with my relationship with my father.' She went to group therapy on Monday evenings. Arthur had a WAEADA meeting at the same time. He was a leading member, along with his friend Angus, of the West Avon Estate Agents, Dealers and Auctioneers.

Unfaithful! What an absurd word – a concept, not the description of an act. Yet it's the concept that does the hurting, not the deed itself. Does infidelity as such matter? Jane going round breaking plates matters; Jane's hair going grey before its time matters; Natalie not caring about the way she makes Jane break plates matters; the way both women use Arthur to reinforce their view of themselves matters. But Natalie leaning her head against Arthur's Antiquax-impregnated jacket and receiving comfort – that matters too, righting scales, and so does the excitement and the thrill of adultery – they *matter*. They're wonderful. Doesn't Natalie's pleasure somehow make up for Jane's grief?

No wonder I, Sonia, am shut up in a madhouse waiting, even as I write, for an injection to stop me twitching and shouting. Trying to establish a moral framework for our existence, to decide exactly who to blame for what, and why, is enough to drive a sane woman mad, and a mad one even madder. In the meantime just accept that though I'm diagnosed as both insane and dangerous, and am a convicted arsonist, my intentions are of the best. My search after truth is absolute. In the telling of this story I am bending over backwards to be fair to absolutely everyone.

So, the wages of sin and the pleasures of adultery now discussed if not quite settled, let's get on with the story.

I'll try and keep out of it, I promise you, except in the third person.

Dinner

Natalie didn't tell the children anything about the rumour that their father had run off with a beauty queen. She was not that kind of mother. Now me, I used to tell my children everything, because there was no one else to tell and I'm a blabbermouth. This may be part of the reason they've taken the children away from me. People think kids ought to be spared the truth: it really upsets them when they're not. Though I don't see why the mere fact of their childhood should earn them this special concession. What happens happens; and when the bailiffs come what's the use of telling the children it's the ratcatcher? The television goes and the rats stay, and the kids are the first to notice. But that's another story.

What Natalie did, on the way home from Coombe Barrow School, was to pass me, Sonia, filing home with my three little girls, Teresa, Bess and Edwina. And she actually stopped to give us a lift. Too late for me to lift the curse, of course, but better than nothing.

Young Ben was horrified at his mother's act of kindness. Young Ben, at twelve, looked like his father, admired his father and made a special effort to be like his father. He had really enjoyed life in the Gambia, where Harrix had operated when he was small. But then his father had packed up and come home rather suddenly: it doesn't do in some countries to leave too many bills unpaid. Ben had really appreciated swimming pools and servants and the sense of superiority that being white gives a child. (It had just made his

mother feel too hot and absurdly pink and sweaty).
Alice had been rather more in favour of coming home.
Alice was a softie: she'd wept at the sight of flies
crawling over babies' eyes.

'They're not *like* us,' Ben would say. 'They don't *feel*
it. Do shut up, Alice.' But she hadn't. Now, back in
England, she wept at the thought of battery hens,
though she went on eating chicken. What it came down
to was that Alice would weep at anything. Some will,
some won't. Ben was right: she was a softie.

Now picture the scene, as I try to, impartially. (Practise looking in, my psychiatrist says, on your own life.
Not looking out. See yourself as others see you!) Teresa,
Bess and Edwina piled into the back seat next to Ben
and Alice, and Sonia eased her pneumatic bulk in next
to Natalie. Sonia didn't eat more than anyone else.
Honestly. It was just depression and unhappiness
made her blow up. (I know what he's going to say
even before he says it. 'Blow up?' my shrink will say.
'Interesting you should use that word. Perhaps what
you're talking about is not depression after all, not
unhappiness, but rage.' Too bad!) Right or wrong, and
be that as it may, Sonia, once an eight-stone stripling,
was now a twelve-stone bubble. Now let's overhear the
conversation.

'This *is* good of you,' said Sonia, trying not to sound
sarcastic. 'I suppose the dog is all right with the children?' Jax, who usually looked steadfastly out of the
back of the car, had turned his head to look at the
invaders of his territory and was baring his teeth.

'Perfectly all right,' said Natalie, her eyes on the road.

'He's baring his teeth,' observed Sonia.

'That's only his smile,' said Natalie, wondering why
she had bothered to pick up Sonia. That 'the under-
privileged were always ungrateful' was one of Harry's

27

maxims. 'If you want a kick in the teeth,' he'd say, 'go out and help someone.'

'If that's his smile,' said Sonia, 'I wouldn't like to see him scowl.'

'Could I ask you something?' said Natalie.

'Ask away.'

'It's about social security,' said Natalie.

'And what makes you think I know anything about social security?' demanded Sonia. She wasn't easy, by any means. Why should she be? 'Does it show in my clothes, or something? Do I walk like a supplicant? No? Well, don't apologize. As it just so happens, I do know a thing or two. Why do you want to know? Is it for a fancy-dress party? Are you dressing up, or rather down, as someone on the dole? Second-hand clothes, that's all you need. You can borrow some of mine if you like.'

'I just wondered,' said Natalie, patiently, 'where the offices were. I can't seem to find them in the telephone book.'

'You look under DHSS' said Sonia. 'Department of Health and Social Security. You don't know much, do you?'

'Not really, no,' said Natalie.

'If you take me first left and then second right, you'll be in Boxover Estate,' said Sonia. 'You can drop us there.' Natalie had to take Sonia right to her front door, in spite of being so low in petrol. Sonia lived at no. 19 Wendover, Boxover: one of a row of small modern homes, each no different to the last, except that the front garden of no. 19 was perhaps more dilapidated than the others, and strewn with children's toys.

'The most boring place on earth,' said Sonia, unwedging herself from the front seat, 'but my home!

28

Thanks for the lift. Any time you want to pick my brains, feel free.'

'Why do people like that always live in such a mess?' asked Ben on the way home. 'It doesn't cost them anything just to tidy it up, does it? But they'd rather live off the rest of us than lift a finger for themselves.'

As his father spoke, so spoke Ben. And you might well think the lad was better off without him; but I don't know: a father's a father, no matter what political sentiments he has.

Sonia waved goodbye to the Volvo and went inside her slovenly home, given to her by courtesy of a benign if querulous state.

That is to say, I went inside. Now my shrink is a grave and amiable fellow and on the whole I trust him. I am doing my best to relate me now, idle and childless, to the 'me' of then, the one who fed and dressed and lived around, by, with and from Teresa, Bess and Edwina. But such a thing is difficult if only because, apart from anything else, the woman without children is so very different from the woman with. And to practise 'objectivity', to third-personalize, which he likes me to do, may well reduce the ego, but it doesn't half fracture one's sense of continuing identity, already seriously threatened. I hope he knows what he's doing. The shrink, incidentally, hates being referred to as a shrink. Why do I wish to diminish him, he asks? Why do I wish to make him cosy and familiar, as if the world were a neat, clean, jokey place, not the fearful nexus of chaos we know it to be? My words, not his. He's not a 'fearful nexus of chaos' man. These things are important, is all he says. That, and 'continue with the creative writing therapy. It's worked for others, why not with you?'

Well, I could tell him. I have monsters inside my

head, with slavering fangs and blood-red eyes, out of whose mouths devils pour, and I daresay the others he speaks of haven't. I do my best to keep things light, for his sake. That's why I go on calling him 'shrink' – to diminish the monsters, not him. And as for 'important'! What does he know about important? He has a proper computer inside his head, lucky man; inside my head are heaps of dead babies over which naked old ladies swarm like maggots, and pits piled with charring bones into which living babies fall and are lost. I don't tell him about the charnel house, which is our real existence, and of which I have arcane knowledge. He'll go to heaven or he'll go to hell, and since he's probably going to heaven he need never know about the other. Why should I upset him by telling him? I am an arsonist and a murderer, or at any rate a woman-slaughterer: they'll never let me out of here. I should be grateful that he talks to me so much. He doesn't have to. Do you know, after all that happened, all my efforts, Teresa, Bess and Edwina went to live with their father? I expect they're happy. Little girls need their daddy. I hope he's told them I'm dead, that's all, so they don't think I'm callously neglecting my maternal duties. I would practise them were I in a position to do so.

So, where are we? Dinner time!

Dinner Time

That evening Sonia – she of the three children – and Natalie were at their respective cookers. Sonia was cooking potatoes, kale and sausages; Natalie was preparing roast chicken and potatoes, and a chocolate mousse made from a packet mix. Natalie had no cooking style whatever. Potatoes and kale can be quite delicious – the secret is to pressure-cook the kale, which reduces its obstinate toughness to quite acceptable stringiness. The flavour's always great. Sonia was fortunate enough to have a pressure-cooker left over from the days when she was married to Stephen the school-teacher, the children's father. That was before she fell in love with Alec the solicitor; married, of course. Stephen left her when he discovered her *in flagrante delicto* and never forgave her; but Alec didn't leave his wife, oh no, which is how Sonia happened to be living off the State's munificence, with three small children. What else was she to do?

'I'm not going to subsidize a whore!' said Stephen, when the question of maintenance arose. He was an upright man, albeit a declared atheist – but when were men ever rational? – leaving his job so he couldn't be required to subsidize her by law.

'You can't get blood out of a stone' ought to be the motto over every DHSS office. Some 60 per cent of men required by law to make maintenance payments make none. About 40 per cent of men are strangely enough better off after a divorce than before, while 80 per cent of divorced women with dependent children are 60 per

31

cent worse off. The statistics are approximate, but you do see what I'm getting at?

Sonia, Teresa, Bess and Edwina ate a lot of lentils and potatoes and the occasional frozen chicken leg, and vitamin C tablets bought in bulk from Boots the Chemist. Sonia wasn't daft. Well, not then, anyway, unless that's what the abandoning of your own life for your children can be called. Without Teresa, Bess and Edwina, Sonia could have been free and thin again. Run off, got a job (well, with any luck. Four million unemployed; but a woman can usually get a job, can't she, if only cleaning up after someone else – look at Flora), gone to the pub, found herself a man and started all over again – even a new family, a little Timothy, Bob and Edward perhaps? She was still young enough. But no, love held her fixed. Love for her children, for Alec, love for Stephen – though none of it had done her much good. The pressure-cooker had been expensive in its time. But the rubber ring round the lid was beginning to perish. Would Sonia ever have the spare cash to buy another? Would she have the energy to seek one out? Probably not. The ring would cost two pounds twenty-seven pence. She could soon recoup its cost in saved electricity. But the poor don't think like that. They can't. They never have the two pounds twenty-seven pence to spare *right now*. That is why, if you ask me, the poor get poorer, the rich richer.

Natalie was in a fix, wasn't she? It was Harry's idea that they should give a dinner party and now it looked as if she was going to be giving it on her own. She wondered whether she should telephone the guests and say she was ill, and cancel the evening; but that would be giving too much credence to her own doubts. No, she would simply get on with it. Half past six would come; Harry would either turn up or he wouldn't; she would give it to seven o'clock, and then surely she would know one way or another; and since the guests were coming at 7.30 (people dine early in the country – they begin yawning at eight and long for bed by ten) that would not be long enough for her to get hysterical. She could see it would be as well for her to be in company, even though she would not trust that company with her confidence.

She hadn't wanted the dinner party. She'd been nervous. But now she was glad.

'But, Harry,' she said, 'it's so long since I've done anything like that. And certainly not without servants.'

'Arthur Wandle and Angus Field run everything round here,' Harry said. 'They might be useful.'

What could Natalie do? Say 'Sorry, it would be embarrassing to have Arthur's wife; I'm having this affair with her husband, you see?' No.

'The antique dealer and the estate agent?' was all she said. 'How can they run everything?'

'They're hand in glove,' was all he said.

Hand in glove! Robber barons was what Harris meant. Buying and selling, property and land, jobs for the boys on the Town Council, drinking with the planners in the pub – nothing went on Arthur and Angus didn't know about, nothing happened they didn't want to see happen. This new garage, that new job. That medieval cottage someone had forgotten to list, vanished overnight. Too late for protest, then; every ancient brick not so much dumped as sold, gone, vanished. Where to? California, some said, where what is old is valued. Smiles, winks and nods. By the way, when I say that Arthur and Jane lived above the shop, let it be said the shop was a sixteenth-century building nestling at the foot of Gurney Castle with a view over the moat and one of the most desirable buildings in all

33

Eddon Gurney, and a grade one listed building besides. There are shops and shops, I can tell you!

Now while Natalie, neatly contained by the right angles and smooth walls of her modern bungalow, inexpertly roasted her boring chickens and tried to blank her mind off from disagreeable probabilities, Arthur and Jane changed for dinner in their beamed and wooded bedroom. The floor sloped badly, and the old oak floorboards had shrunk in the central heating; if Jane wore high heels she was in danger of twisting her ankle. The furniture here changed frequently: Arthur would sell even his wife's dressing table if a customer had a mind to it: and there would frequently be a gap until it was replaced. The floor of the very beautiful eighteenth-century Dutch wardrobe had never been properly fixed, and would collapse at intervals, so Arthur's shoes would often be in a tumble on the floor. They were today. It made him cross. Being turned down by Natalie had irritated him. He thought probably the affair was over. He quite looked forward to Tuesdays and Thursdays, but not enough. Natalie had no conversation: she was like the Victorian dolls his wife collected (she would: a sentimentalist), all wide eyes, smooth cold skin and silent blinking. If one laid them on their backs, their eyes closed.

Jane put on a flowered dress he hated. It bunched around her waist. Nothing was really satisfactory.

'Why did you accept the invitation?' It was in the nature of a complaint rather than a question.

'I didn't,' she said, startled into protest. 'You did.'

'I'd rather stay home and watch TV,' said Arthur, 'than sit about with local tradesmen.'

'The Harrises aren't local,' Jane said. 'They come from somewhere in Africa.'

'They're the kind who buy new furniture and polish

34

it with Sparkle.' It was the worst thing he could say of anyone. 'Harry Harris will talk about computers and his wife about schools.'

'Angus and Jean are going,' said Jane, in her best placating voice. She was the kind of wife who looks out of her front door in the morning and, if it's raining, apologizes.

'Angus will fall asleep, and Jean will look down her nose,' said Arthur, not placated at all. It seemed to him that Angus was nosing ahead in their race to the top. Arthur lived above the shop; Angus a mile or so outside the town, in a Georgian house with three acres. Balance that against the fact the shop was a listed building of major historical interest and that the house had been bought cheap as bankrupt stock (from a man Angus had bankrupted, but never mind): in Arthur's mind Angus was winning. Arthur, this particular evening when nothing seemed right, didn't like the thought of that at all. He, Arthur, had a wife who twitched and heard children reading: Angus' wife Jean was a qualified pharmacist and worked in the local Boots. Mind you, Jean didn't seem to care about Angus; just raised her eyebrows and talked to him as if he were a child. Arthur could at least make his wife weep, and took comfort from the fact.

Natalie watched the hands of the clock reach six, then half past six. Harry didn't arrive home. She gave the children the last of the fishfingers from the bottom of the freezer. A pity, she thought, she hadn't stocked up when she could. The table was laid for six. Arthur and Jane, Angus and Jean, herself and Harry: proof that they could now count themselves as part of the business community. She had laid out the smoked salmon and cut thin slices of buttered brown bread and even thinner slices of lemon. She had timed the chickens for nine o'clock: they were ready sprinkled with dried rosemary as the recipe book had suggested. Peeled potatoes were waiting in cold water. The frozen peas were decanted into the pan. A bread sauce mix waited in the bowl for its re-hydration. The chocolate mousse had been made and Ben and Alice had quarrelled over who should lick the spoon and who should scrape the bowl.

The table was exceptionally prettily laid, with white linen napkins folded into bird-like shapes and placed in the tall wine glasses. The napkins were the only ones of Natalie's possessions which linked her back to the past at all, the art of folding them the only traditional skill she had. The napkins had been her mother's. They had been small enough and flat enough to pack and go around the world: they had never been lost. And the art of folding, just so, had been taught to her grandmother by her great-great aunt, back in the summer of 1912. The bird shapes seemed unnecessarily ornate on an otherwise simple table – she worried about their suitability. She wondered if there were people in the world who did not worry about things. I could have told her, but that was in the days before she said the thoughts out loud. She kept them inside, and they kept her dead.

'Where's Daddy?' Ben asked, at seven o'clock. 'He said he'd be back at six-thirty. He's always punctual. I set my watch by him.' He didn't, of course, but he liked the ring of the phrase.

'He's been delayed,' said Natalie. She had put on her best blue dress with the wide white collar. Now she peered in the bedroom mirror, bevelled around the edges, and put on her eye make-up. That was blue, too. Women should never wear blue – it's too innocent a colour. I remember as a child there was a colour called nigger brown: that was almost as bad: not innocent, simply dreary. Of course the phrase has gone out of fashion. Down here in the West Country they wouldn't understand why, or approve if they did. No one but puffy pale pinkos in sight down here, and racism's rampant. In this respect the heart of the country is mean, and spiteful, and frightened.

'People should do what they say they'll do,' said Ben, going back to the television. He was doing his maths homework at the same time as watching the screen, which he was not supposed to do.

'But perhaps he's had an accident,' said Alice, and her blue eyes opened wide with fancied horror.

'He rang earlier and said he might have to go up to London,' said Natalie, 'on urgent business.' She was trying out the excuses she would offer to her guests. 'Perhaps he's had a breakdown on the motorway; or his client's flight was delayed.'

'But the car's just been serviced,' said Ben. 'And if it was a question of delay, surely the meeting would simply be rescheduled?' He would sometimes get up really early and watch the business management courses, screened by the Open University.

'We'll wait and see,' said Natalie, vaguely. But it was now 7.15 and she could see that Hilary had been right. Harry had done a bunk. She went up to her bedroom and opened the clever little jewellery box which played Schubert's lullaby when she opened it and slid out all its drawers when she lifted the inner lid – Harry had given it to her one Christmas – and found her diamond ring gone and her amber necklace. All that was left was junk jewellery. She put on a pair of cheap hoop earrings and stared at herself, and thought they suited her quite well.

'Don't wear those earrings,' said Alice, when she went downstairs, 'they make you look like a gypsy.'

'I'll look like what I want!' snapped Natalie, uncharacteristically. She took a swig of whisky, and tried to relocate herself, as it were, in her own skin. She felt as if she was in a corner of the room somewhere, watching her body move and act, but scarcely residing in it.

She would have liked to have cried, but with guests expected for dinner, how could she? Her eyes would be red and puffy if she indulged her feelings.

Meanwhile, Jean, Angus' wife, the pharmacist, was tugging on a tight black suede skirt over thin hips. Then she pulled on a light fluffy blue angora jumper. She had thin shoulders and no breasts to speak of. Angus watched, and Jean was indifferent to his watching. She was dark and cross and seldom smiled, and he was plump and fair and smiled a lot, even as he stabbed you in the back. He wished he was married to the kind of wife who would fancy sex as she changed for dinner, but he wasn't.

'I'm hungry,' Angus said, as he changed out of his auctioneer's tweedy suit into the smooth grey suit he wore for evening occasions. 'You don't think she'll cook cuisine minceur?'

'Fat hope,' she said. 'Actually we'll be lucky if there's any dinner at all.'

'Why's that?' he asked.

Now Jean loved dropping bombshells. Sometimes he thought she kept him for the sake of dropping them and watching him jump, in the same way as some people keep dogs in order to watch them sit up and beg.

'Harrix went bust,' she told him, as if she were mentioning that the cat had been sick.

'Who said so?' His hand stilled as he fumbled for buttons. Fool and joker he might be: king of the country he was. Ordinary intelligence – the talk in pubs and offices – had failed him. He needed to know.

'Mrs Barnes came in after evening surgery for some Diezepan – said her husband was out of work again. So was everyone else up at Harrix.'

'But he had a million-pound order on the books.'

'So he said,' said Jean. 'More fool you to believe him. Do you want to call and cancel dinner? I don't imagine Harris is much use to you now.'

But he didn't. He was hungry. If he stayed home Jean would give him a boiled egg and some salad and lecture him on cholesterol.

'Tell me more,' he said. But she wouldn't. She would feed him scraps of information as she fed him sight of her breasts, for the pleasure of snatching satisfaction away. 'I don't want to get a name for gossip,' she said, 'or they'll stop telling me things. You're putting on weight,' she added, not failing to notice that he had to tug at his belt to get it to his normal hole.

Only when they were in the car – a new Audi Quattro, with every modern gadget available, including a bleeper which went off if you exceeded the speed limit you set yourself, of which Angus was extremely proud – did Jean say: 'What's more, Mrs Hopfoot came in for Mogadon. She said her daughter had run off with Harry Harris. You know, that blonde girl with the good legs but the screwed-up face? I think perhaps a harelip, not very well fixed. Some said it gave her charm, but I never could see it.'

'You're having me on,' he said. 'You're joking.'

'If it isn't true, Harry Harris will be sitting at the head of the table, and if it is true, he won't,' she said, staring ahead from behind glasses upswept at the corners, with her wide West Country eyes, full of innocence and savagery mixed; and he thought perhaps she wasn't joking.

A little later she said:

'Of course, you can't blame Harry Harris too much, considering what his wife's like.'

'What's his wife like?'

'She's been having it off with Arthur, on Tuesday and Thursday afternoons, back of the shop.'

'I don't believe you!' But he did. He went too fast round a corner and had to brake sharply. The bleeper sounded and he had to grope for the switch to turn it off.

'I suppose you envy Arthur,' his wife remarked. And then, as if by the way, 'Idiotic car, isn't it! Why did you buy it? All it does is make you look a fool. It's too big and too flash; it uses too much petrol and it's impossible to park. You're such a baby. You think people admire you and envy you for your fancy new car, but they don't. All they think is, there goes a man with more money than sense.'

'What's the matter with you?' he asked. 'Fancy Arthur yourself?'

She yawned, artificially.

'If I was going to fancy anyone,' she said, 'I'd fancy a twenty-year-old, not a middle-aged antique dealer.'

'Fun evening this is going to be,' was all he could think of to say.

It wasn't, of course. Conversation was stilted. Harry Harris was indeed missing. Natalie said he'd gone to London unexpectedly that morning, and had rung from a garage to say he'd broken down on the motorway. No one believed her, but no one said they didn't. There wasn't enough smoked salmon. It was impossible to squeeze the lemon. The chickens had dried out. Jean

refused the chocolate mousse on account of the cholesterol it contained. Natalie nearly said it came from a
packet and was a special low-calorie brand, favoured
by Harry, but stopped herself in time. Jane looked as
if she were about to burst into tears. The only thing of
interest that happened – apart from the negative fact
of Harry's absence – was that Angus admired Natalie's
hoop earrings; it occurred to him that she was just the
sort of woman who would enjoy ten minutes' sex while
changing for dinner, or even twenty minutes, and if
she saw something in Arthur she might see even more
in him, Angus. What's more, if Harry had gone
missing, he, Angus, might be able to help her out.

Angus pinched Natalie's bottom in the kitchen, going
out to help her fetch another bottle of wine – she'd kept
the red in the fridge, and taken out the white to warm:
well, she was distracted – and she slapped his hand
away. Had the instinct for self-preservation been
predominant in her mind, she would have welcomed
the bruise left by those powerful and monied and possibly helpful fingers. As it was, he was hurt, and never
quite forgave her, not in all that came after. Natalie
carried some kind of female aura around with her; she
carried it like a suitcase: it was fixed to her and yet not
part of her, a burden and a delight. It was impersonal
and it made men want her to smile at them, and
rendered them very irritable if she didn't.

It wasn't only men Natalie affected like this: it was
women too. Look how I cursed her when she splashed
me, driving by like Lady Muck: she with the debts and
the runaway husband and not a true friend to her
name, only the kind of business acquaintance who'd
come to dinner and gossip about her behind her back,
and fuck her out of turn, or try to. For love read hate.
I brought it all down on her: or the demons in my head

did. They feed on love and spew out hate. The more hope there is, the stronger they get. Flat depression, flat despair, is easier. Take my word for it.

Our dinner that night up at the housing estate consisted of kale and potatoes with a few scraps of sausage stirred in. Teresa, Bess and Edwina ate it without argument and afterwards we all watched Top of the Pops. When I look back on that time it seems happy enough – compared at any rate to now. I blame Natalie for what happened.

My shrink says I am prepared to blame everyone except myself for my fate. If I practised understanding and sympathy more, he says, I might blame less, and be the happier for it. More brutally, if I learned not to hate myself, I might not hate others, and then he might even let me out of the madhouse. He is ever hopeful! He thinks arson (one of my crimes, or madnesses) is a declaration of hate. I think arson is a pretty fine idea, one way and another. Fire is beautiful. What it burns is dross, rubbish; it eats up ugliness: it devours the debris of lost hope: it obliterates the imperfect. The ashes from a really good fire are soft, young and fine. I loved Natalie. I didn't wish her any harm. When her troubles came upon her, how the vultures moved in! Then for a time, I was her only friend. It was she who betrayed me, not the other way round. If to want happiness for yourself is to be guilty, then, yes, I am guilty. But I am not full of hate and rage, on the contrary. I wish I was – then I could see a way out of this dismal place.

Shuffling ladies in shapeless cardigans are forever bringing me cups of over-sugared tea, which it would seem churlish to refuse. They ask me why I write instead of joining in their singsongs, and I just nod and smile and they seem not to notice that I haven't answered. Someone did once ask *what* I was writing and I replied 'Just therapy' and she said 'Novel or autobiography?' and I was at a loss to reply. Not that it mattered; she shook her double chins at me and drifted off, like anyone else. It's the drugs produce the double chins. But none of my questioners seems to have any teeth. Can this be the result of too much tannin? How bad people are at looking after themselves!

That was dinner, anyway, on the night of the day Harry Harris left for work, and never came home.

Chomp, Chomp, Grittle-Grax, Gone!

The fox was out that night. It got Ros' duckling. Ros lives across the road from me in Wendover Drive. The duckling was a pretty little thing. It had been reared by her two daft hens. One of her kids had found this still warm duck's egg under a hedge, and since Ros' hens spent every spring and summer broody, without ever so much as laying an egg in return for their keep, she put the blue egg where a single addled white shop egg had rested for six weeks or so and look, folks, it hatched! How excited we all were! Silly little cheeping, trusting, mismatched creature. Small things please small minds: us, that is, up in the housing estate. Those of us who live off the State get smaller and smaller minds. We don't take the newspapers, perhaps that's it. Then the fox got the duckling. Ros' children cried. So did Teresa, Bess and Edwina. I could have wrung its neck. The duckling's, not the fox's. The duckling stirred delight in us, who had no business to be delighted; we, the rejects of the system, the rejects of marriage, the unsupported mothers who live off the State. Cheep, cheep, it went: saved by a miracle, hatched by besotted elderly spinsters, it made us think that nice things still could happen. I don't blame the fox. It only acted according to its nature. Chomp, chomp, grittle-grax, gone!

Natalie told me she saw it, or its brother, run across her lawn. After the guests had gone she was putting out the rubbish in her bin – she was like that: never left waste until the morning – when the fox ran across

44

her back lawn. She saw it in the light which shone out from her kitchen. It stopped and stared at her with its red eyes, seeming quite unafraid, and then loped on.

Foxes have a nasty habit of killing everything in the henhouse and leaving the debris behind and the straw and the walls spattered by blood and feather. They like to kill, not just to eat, or so the story goes. But every creature has its defenders, and I heard someone say on the radio the other day that the fox is not really blood-crazed: it's just that its instincts can't cope with walls. In the wild its victims would all have run off before it could get to them. I leave that for you to think about.

Anyway, the elderly hens couldn't run off. The fox got them too. The duckling just vanished, but bits of hen were everywhere. Well, they'd done their bit, I suppose. What good's an old hen that doesn't lay eggs, any more than a woman too old or too cut about to have children? I was sterilized after Edwina. Stephen thought it a good idea. Three little girls in as many years, after ten years of trying and nothing. Delicious at the time! But where was it going to end? And then, I don't know, it was as if my non-pregnancy or perpetual pregnancy was the only solder that kept us interested in each other. When I wasn't in the market for babies and sex was for sex's sake Stephen just seemed to lose interest. Then I fell in love with Alec, our solicitor, and Stephen acted as if he were Othello and I was Desdemona, only I'd recovered from the strangling and absolutely spoiled the play. And if you ask me it was my hysterectomized state which prevented Alec from taking me seriously. What man wants a woman without a womb, any more than he wants a woman with a womb that age has dried up? It goes against nature.

Mind you, it was said in my defence at the trial that my hysterectomy had preyed upon my mind. I pleaded guilty but insane and the plea was accepted. I must have been mad. All you have to do with a prison term is just sit it out and it comes to an end, and you go home – or whatever's left of home after you've been out of it for a decade or so. But if you get sent to a psychiatric hospital, or 'loonybin' as we who know them still call them, you only get out if and when some psychiatrist swears you are now sane. And who's ever going to swear that about another human being? Chomp, chomp, grittle-grax, gone! Ros' duckling and me, but not Natalie. Natalie proved too tough for predators.

Anyway, as I was saying. The guests went home and Natalie was about to put the chicken bones in the bin, when she realized there was nothing to eat for tomorrow's dinner. She took the debris back inside, filled a saucepan with water, put the bones in, then scraped the plates into the pan as well, including a bit of gristle chewed and rejected by Jean – Natalie was sure she was as healthy as a human being could be – put the lid on tight and boiled up the lot before she went to bed. She would serve it tomorrow for dinner, as soup. She was learning.

She dreaded going to bed, but in fact fell immediately and soundly asleep, and had no dreams, or at any rate none that she could recall.

'Where's Daddy?' Alice asked, first thing.

'Dad will really have to speak to that garage,' said Ben. 'It's too bad.'

He spoke in his father's voice, and Natalie had to refrain from slapping him. I am not saying that Natalie did not love her children: merely remarking that it is easier to love a child who is the fruit of passionately desired loins, if you see what I mean, than to love a child to whose begetter you are indifferent or whom you actively dislike. And Natalie had never been passionate about Harry's loins.

They used to believe that love children – that is to say, children born out of wedlock – were always beautiful; a romantic view, of course, presupposing village love, not sordid urban accident by way of proximity or drunkenness, and not statistically viable; but it is something, I suppose, that people want to believe. Teresa, Bess and Edwina are good-looking enough. Regular features, good teeth. Though Edwina has (or had, when I last saw her – their father does not let them visit) those rather sad screwed-up little eyes which children get when they have suffered too many blows from fate. Perhaps now she is with her father and not her mad, bad mother they will begin to look more confidently at the world. (Self, self, self, Sonia. You'll never get out at this rate.)

'Your father's away on business,' said Natalie to Ben and Alice. What else could she say? It had a convincing enough ring: the nice impenetrability of the male reason for being off and out of the home. Away on business! What business? Where? They didn't ask.

Now Natalie's Volvo, with its pitiful pool of petrol in the tank, and the yellow warning light not just flickering but full on for the last eight miles, was parked in front of the house. The garage, kept for Harry's Cortina, stood empty, with only a dusty spot or two of oil to mark the place where it ought to be, at 8 o'clock in the morning. Jax was hungry. Natalie found a can of bolognese sauce at the back of the cupboard and fed him that. He looked reproachful but ate it.

'I don't know what Dad would say,' said Ben, 'if he saw you do that. What a wicked waste of money!'

'Dad isn't here to say anything,' said Natalie, and somewhere from the back of her mind, creeping out from under the thick wodge of stupor that seemed to fill it, came the notion, like a thread of silk in a flannel cloth, that being able to do what you liked, as you liked, without comment, might be a pleasant thing. That, in fact, there might be life beyond marriage.

Alice came out in alarm from her bedroom. From her window she could see two men in suits coming up the drive. They had left their Ford Escort in the road, where it was causing quite an obstruction; but they didn't seem to care. One tried the driver's door of the Volvo and, finding it open, got in and started the engine: it whirred, then died.

'Mummy,' cried Alice, 'someone's stealing the car!'

But of course they were merely repossessing it. Harry had not kept up the payments. They showed Natalie documents which she did not understand.

'It won't start,' said the would-be driver, reproachfully.

'There'll be trouble if the vehicle is damaged in any way,' said his companion. They seemed unmoved by Natalie's wide, troubled eyes and pale face. She was not used to that. Did one lose the power to affect men, along with a husband?

'It's out of petrol, that's all,' she said, and they got a can of petrol out of the Escort, fed the Volvo and drove it out.

'You are a fool,' said Ben. 'You shouldn't have told them that. Then they'd have had to have gone away and Dad would have come back and sorted it out. He's going to be ever so angry.'

'How are we going to get to school?' asked Alice.

'By taxi, idiot,' said Ben.

'We're going to walk,' said Natalie. 'It's a lovely morning.'

'Walk!' said Ben, speaking as one who has no legs. 'I can't possibly!'

'Then stay home,' said Natalie, briefly, so he went away to pack his books and came back to say the handle of his briefcase was broken and he had to have a new one that very day. Natalie told him he could keep his books in a plastic bag and he snorted his derision. He was upset about the seizure of the car. Who wouldn't be?

'It's like *The Railway Children*,' said Alice. 'We're reading it at school. Their father's falsely accused and goes to prison and then they're very poor and have adventures.'

'You're so stupid!' said Ben, and pulled her hair. So Alice went for Ben with her nails and Natalie slapped both their faces so hard it actually hurt, and after that they behaved. She, who never slapped children, beginning to behave like the rest of us! Distraught + distracted + dismayed = slaps and shrieks.

Natalie stood numbed and carless in her kitchen when the back door pushed open and there stood – no, not Harry, but Angus. He carried a dead hen by its legs.

'Excellent dinner last night,' he said. 'Thought I'd drop by and say thank you in person.'

'It was a horrible dinner,' she said. 'The chickens were dry. Fish and chips from the Chinese takeaway would have been nicer.' Yes, Chinese takeaways have reached even as far as Eddon Gurney, Somerset.

'I thought I might have missed you,' he said. 'Your car's not there.'

'It's having a service,' she said, not even sure why she lied.

'Funny,' he said. 'I thought I passed it on the road.

Being driven by a man I know. Works for a hire-purchase company.'

'Can't have been,' she said.

'Harry's car's not in the garage either,' said Angus. 'He's off early.'

'Yes, isn't he?' she said. She didn't like Angus. He was too fair and fleshy for her taste.

'Have it your own way,' he said. 'Do you want a chicken? Fox left it.'

There was a drop of blood upon her tiled floor.

Natalie thought once, twice, thrice.

'Thank you,' she said, and Angus put the dead bird, feathers and all, in her fridge. Why does he feel so much at home, she wondered? Coming in without knocking, opening her fridge without so much as an if you please. I told her the answer later. Men have a group consciousness, just as ants do. If one falls off the shelf another fills the gap. It's only natural, especially if there's honey around.

'Your fridge is almost empty,' he said. 'Not a pretty sight. I reckon you'll be needing some help, girl.'

'I'm perfectly all right,' said Natalie.

'Have it your own way,' he said. 'How are you getting the kids to school?'

'We're walking.'

'I'll give you a lift.'

'It's a fine morning. We often walk.'

'You've got friends, I suppose? Family?'

'Of course I have.' But she hadn't. And whose fault was that? She shouldn't have looked down her nose at the likes of Pauline, not to mention me, Sonia. She should have written to aunts who sent her birthday cards. She'd thought herself too good for too many people, said 'I prefer the company of men' once too often. Pride comes before a fall; a sense of sisterhood with sad experience.

'I'll be off then,' he said. 'Give Harry my regards when he gets back. We missed him last night.'

She didn't reply.

'I expect you did too,' he added, laughing. She stared at him unblinking. 'Anyway,' he added, 'Arthur will always look after you. Good fellow, Arthur.'

This time she did blink, which gratified him enough to allow him to leave.

First things first. Get the children to school, then face the day. Picture the scene: Natalie shepherding her two children along the side of the main road, along which she was so blithely accustomed to drive. Ben's right cheek is unduly pink, as is Alice's left. Natalie herself is pale, in spite of her good night's sleep. Sonia sees her walking ahead, and hurries Teresa, Bess and Edwina along to catch up with her. In so doing she changes her life.

Ros Sweeney from over the way had told Sonia that morning that Marion Hopfoot had run off with Natalie Harris' husband. Sonia had been partly appalled and partly gratified that Natalie had left the wives and joined the women; and was certainly awed by the rapid working of her curse. She wanted to be in, moreover, at the kill. Not nice!

Now it is Sonia's shrink's belief that in this new world of ours, in which what happens on a TV screen is accepted as more real than life itself, and certainly more true to the truth of experience, that the way to deal with personal trauma is to project painful scenes – the ones we'd prefer just to forget – onto the screens of our minds, and so learn to accept and incorporate the negative aspects of our personalities. To see ourselves as not central to our own experience, as it were, but an inevitable part of a larger interweaving drama. It does seem to work. I, Sonia, in replaying the last scene, can now see that in believing my curse worked, I was merely trying to edge nearer the centre of a stage that is not mine by rights. I am not omnipotent and to know that is to be relieved of a good deal of guilt. Next time I am handed a cup of sweet tea I will mention that I don't take sugar. Such are the wages of a clear conscience. You begin to be able to look after yourself.

There were eight of us on the carnival float the day it caught fire. That was in November. Natalie's husband left in March, when the daffodils were springing. Odd about daffodils, don't you think? A delight in the New Year, rare, forced and pale: boring and oppressive by April, when they're everywhere, too bright and cheap. Even I sometimes buy a bunch in April, when the greengrocers are almost paying you to take them out of their sight. In my great days – for that's how I now see the days when I was reckoned sane – I used to get a total of fifty-two pounds thirty-two pence a week from social security for me and the three kids. You can't often afford shop flowers on that, and you don't have the energy or will to pick wild ones from the hedgerows, and stick them in a jam jar. That's what a low income does to you. It makes you punish yourself long after others have stopped doing it. If you're poor, the logic goes in your head, you deserve to be poor. That's if you're a woman, of course. Misfortune makes women feel guilty; men take to rioting in the streets. That's why women in our society are poorer than men by 42 per cent. Or something like that.

I could go on about wild flowers, too: about how rare they've become in the heart of the country, thanks to pesticides, fungicides and weedkiller, but I won't.

Teresa, Bess and Edwina were wild flowers, in their way. Oh, forget it!

This float, this carnival float. The West Country has its own carnival, not like the Rio one, true, but considering the narrowness of the roads and the chilliness of November fairly spectacular. West Avon Estate Agents, Dealers and Auctioneers (Arthur and Angus in disguise) last year entered one of the better floats, and on it, dressed as traditional housewives, in bright, waisted dresses and with frilly aprons, and waving feather dusters at the passing crowd, stood Natalie, Jean, Jane, Sonia, Ros, Sally (whom Sonia hasn't yet told you about), Pauline, and Flora – you remember, Natalie's cleaner? – sitting central and triumphant as the carnival queen. Flora was dressed in old lace, halfway between the old Virgin Mary and the new Madonna, pop star. I don't think any more it was Sonia's fault the float burned: rather it was society's. By 'society' I mean men, for who else forms and regulates the world we live in? Who else but men would dress their wives and mistresses, those they torment, abuse and exploit, in the clothes of the fifties, hand them feather dusters, oblige them to smile and parade the streets of Somerset on a ninety foot float consisting of pretty little estate houses with lace curtains? In a world where something like 40 per cent of women are out at work (and 45 per cent of men), 25 per cent of mothers are on social security, 40 per cent (and rising) are over 60 years of age, how can men still cling to the consoling myth of the loving female in the dream house? Husband out to work, two children at school, mother at home looking after them – that's the rarity these days, not the norm, just 23 per cent of the total of households. No, I'm glad the float burned, it deserved to burn, and though Sonia stays in the loonybin (forgive me, patients, friends, relatives of those incarcerated – sorry, there I go again. No locks and bars these days, just the chemical cosh, the heavy tranquillizers) – stays in the *psychiatric hospital* for ever she's not going to say otherwise.

Sonia's shrink says he reads everything she writes, but Sonia doesn't believe it. Sonia is going to write on, and then smuggle the manuscript out of here and get it to a publisher. They give you paper to write on if its therapy, but not if you're writing fiction. Sometimes Sonia can't remember who's pulling whose leg.

Facing the Day

Sonia made a joke or so that morning, catching up with Natalie on the walk to school. Natalie wasn't particularly talkative. She still had this idea that if you kept yourself to yourself everything would be okay. Slam the front door and keep the world out, was her motto. Only now if she slammed the front door the whole house would shake and fall.

'Car broken down then?' Sonia asked.

'Yes,' said Natalie, conscious of Ben blenching. Obviously it was as he feared, and this embarrassing acquaintance could never now be shaken free. In the file that made its way to school were six females (four of them sponging off the State) and one male, and he was the male. It was a terrible situation. He would be seen, moreover, by friends from school, who were driving past in proper style and comfort, and laughed at. He hated his childhood. It was appalling to be so at the mercy of the adult world: to be obliged to suffer one humiliation after another because of its disinterest or actual sadism. It would have been perfectly possible for his mother to have ordered a taxi and saved him from this ordeal, but she just wouldn't.

'Can't your husband mend the car?' asked Sonia (the bitch!), and her voice floated in the wind over hedges and fields. I will give you a discourse on hedges presently: about layering. Hedges ought to be layered in the winter, not just have their tops sheared by that machinery which is so dangerous to passing traffic. Branches must be bent, part-severed, and intertwined

55

in all but horizontal position, so a calculated and stock-proof tangle of foliage is achieved. The cuts heal, leaves and flowers spring, birds delight, fieldmice rejoice. (You said presently, Sonia, not now. You mean well, then you forget. Part of your difficulty is your capacity to be sidetracked: into, for example, arson: *shrink*)

'No,' said Natalie.

'What do you keep him for then?' asked Sonia. That was the joke. (Shall we consider anti-male humour and what we are really trying to say when we indulge in it?: *shrink*)

Natalie laughed politely. Sonia knew then she wanted something.

'Walking's all right in this weather,' said Sonia. 'It's when it rains and the cars splash you I hate it. Mostly it's the women drivers are the worst. And people who have dogs in the back. I don't know why.'

But Natalie didn't seem to be listening.

'Can you tell me about social security?' was all she asked.

Now she'd come to the right person for that. Sonia was practically a founder member of the Claimants' Union. (Now defunct by reason of encroaching lethargy. My own theory is that they put something in the glue on the back of the brown envelopes circulated by the DHSS.)

'Not between now and nine o'clock, no,' said Sonia. 'Some time perhaps when I've got a week to spare. When I'm dying of malnutrition in the cottage hospital, and have a spare moment from taking the kids to school and back, you come to my bedside and I'll tell you. Not that they usually admit those dying of malnutrition into hospital these days – they'd have no room for proper contributing citizens if they did, would they? But I might swing it through the Claimants' Union. Though, now I come to think of it, they've closed the Cottage Hospital, so you'd have to take the bus into Bristol to visit me: they might give you a special compassionate allowance to pay that, but by then I'd be dead.'

'Seriously though,' said Natalie. She was just a kid herself. She thought I was joking.

'What do you want to know, precisely? Low Income Family Supplement? That's great if you swing it, but you have to find yourself a full-time job first. You can get them round here cleaning the milk tankers. Inside, not out. You crawl around inside them all night for sixty pounds a week. The fumes make you sick all the next day, and may do long term damage to the CNS. Central nervous system, to you. And you're not the type employers are looking for: you might ask for more, little Olivia Twist, or go to the Factory Inspectorate. But you just might be lucky, and actually get the job. Then you could claim a blanket allowance, a whole 50p! Lucky old you. Dog food? No – no pets on the State, I'm afraid. If you're thinking of going on social security, why don't you cook and eat the dog?'

Jax was bringing up the rear of our little procession; did I forget to tell you that? Bess was frightened of him, and I'm not surprised. She kept bumping into my legs while I walked, in her attempts to keep out of the beast's way. I had to keep turning round, and warning her not to go too far out into the centre of the road, where death awaited, not just the fear and exhaustion of walking along its edge.

'So, no pets,' Sonia went on. 'They'll pay for a colour telly though, so the kids can watch monsters, rape and murder and not feel left out. A spot of sexist singing and dancing and a blown-up body or so and a close-up of a child starved to death by its parents on the news. They're stopping subsidized school dinners round here. Presently they'll start handing out a sandwich lunch allowance on a sliding scale, depending on fillings, which will cost more to administer than a free dinner a day for the entire population. That's the way it goes. Does that answer your question about social security, or the DHSS as it is known to connoisseurs?'

'Where are their offices?' she asked. She didn't even know that. My favourite haunt had somehow passed her by.

It's no use. I am guilty. I should never have caught up with Natalie that morning. I should have taken a lesson out of her book and kept myself to myself. I wanted to embarrass her and hurt her by asking about her husband, and I was punished.

By Accident on Purpose

You remember the Sally I mentioned, one of the women who ended up in a frilly dress waving a feather duster at the gawping crowds from a blazing float? She was another one who failed, by-accident-on-purpose to do her best for Natalie. That is to say, she really believed she was doing her best for her unfortunate sister, but her own state of mind got in the way. Since you can never tell what your motives are if you're unhappy, you'd better interfere as little as you can as you go about the world. Or at least do your victims the honour of not trying to justify your actions, once you've done what you've done.

Sally Bains works up at the office of Coombe Barrow School, where the fees are £1,250 a term, in advance, which for Ben and Alice means £2,500 a term, and all of that owing, and more. Sally's married to Valentine. Sally and Val were research scientists until the unit where they both worked closed down for lack of government funding. Val was a world expert in ergot-related diseases of wheat, and Sally knew everything there was to know about fungal diseases in bats. But who cares about either, these days? The money came out of fungi and went into the development of defence mechanisms in outer space – Star Wars to you and me. Too late for Val and Sally to change their disciplines: they were in their forties, with bright young twenty-year-olds who never even stopped to read the newspaper treading hot on their heels. So Sally and Val took their redundancy money, sold their house, and bought

59

a cottage in the West Country, putting what was left into High Risk Commodity shares, which a broker told Val were wrongly named. Low risk to the shrewd, he said, high risk only to the incompetent. First the cottage had to have a new roof – that was two thousand, one hundred pounds – and then eight thousand pounds of Val's money disappeared overnight into some great vat of coffee beans, if you put your hand in which you might pull out a fortune, or more likely lose your hand altogether. Which Val did, so to speak. The day he heard the money had gone, Val stooped to pick up a handkerchief – why didn't he use a tissue like anyone else? Then it would never have happened – and slipped a disc. He was tense, you see. Rest and manipulation failed; an operation exacerbated rather than soothed the trouble, and now Val lay in bed, depressed, and whether he was in pain or merely thought he was in pain, who could tell, and what difference did it make anyway? Meanwhile Sally worked as a secretary at Coombe Barrow, and thought herself lucky.

The trouble with men who suffer from mild clinical depression – that is to say, not quite as bad as the drugged zombies you meet in here – is that they do tend to drink too much and hit their wives in their frustration, and the more their wives try to help the more they are insulted and berated for their pains. Everything's wrong and miserable and awful, and whose fault can it be but the wife's? And since wives tend to take their husband's view of them, they get confused and wretched themselves, not to mention hit, and feel it's their fault their husband's job/back/talent/life has failed, because he keeps saying it is. 'Look how I'm drinking!' he raves. 'Your fault!' 'Who, me?' the startled spouse responds. 'When I've done everything for you all these years! Really me? I suppose it must be, darling, if you say so. How I wish I were nearer what you want, that my breasts were bigger (smaller), my brain was better (worse), that I wasn't so argumentative (acquiescent), then this would never have happened. I can see how it's terrible for you, how my failure has driven you to infidelity. Oh, I am so sorry! Weren't we once happy? What? No? Never? Oh, oh, oh!' She weeps and wails and laments and he lowers through the once happy home, aggrieved and self-righteous. Well, that's how I, Sonia, see it: I put it to the shrink and he agreed, but asked why I couldn't keep my mind on my own problems, which run to the manic rather than the depressive.

As I say, the morning Natalie came up to Sally Bains in the school office Sally herself was distressed and confused. She'd left Val a hump in the bed, with a thermos of coffee beside him for when he woke, and she kissed the top of his head fondly – it was all she could see – and he'd said something and she'd said:

'What did you say, darling?' and he'd said:

'Don't kiss the top of my head. You know you don't mean it,' and she'd said:

'Oh,' feeling as if she'd been slapped, and he'd opened an eye and said:

'Christ. Don't you know better than to put coffee in a thermos? Couldn't you at least give it to me in a cup, like other people?'

And since she was late for work – the making of the coffee had made her late, and the ringing of the doctor for a repeat prescription of painkillers for his back, and the phone had been engaged and engaged and engaged, as it always was in the early morning, she just left. And what's more, he'd had the drawer by the bed open, in which he kept the photograph of the girl he had ditched in order to marry Sally twenty years back. She knew she ought to have stayed and taken away the thermos and made fresh coffee and left that (in a cup and saucer: he didn't like mugs either) by the bed, but somehow that morning she just had to get out. And now she was at the office she was beginning to feel better, only the feeling better was not somehow the true state, was it? It was a kind of frivolity. Other people lived in a cheerful, trivial world which Val did not allow her to inhabit. And Val was right. She knew well enough that coffee never tastes its best after being in a thermos an hour or so; she should have remembered that, instead of how the thermos would let him sleep on, escape from the pain in his back, and still have something hot and reviving to drink when he woke up. She'd got it wrong, as usual.

'Can I ask you something, Mrs Bains?'

'Ask away.' Sally smiled brightly. Sally knew that Harry Harris had run off with Marion Hopfoot the beauty queen. Everyone did. Some cared more than others. Most just thought it a good story.

'How do I go about taking the children out of school? We are just a little financially pushed, and what with the back fees and so forth . . .'

As she spoke Natalie stopped smiling brightly herself, turned quite pale and sat down. She could not quite grasp what she was saying, let alone the sense or otherwise of saying it. One part of her brain was trying to talk to the other, but couldn't get through. It kept ringing engaged. It was a horrible feeling. But look now, rationally, using the brain that *was* attempting to ring through, even if Harry did eventually get in touch, did repent or whatever, did come home, did send a cheque, and it all turned out to be some kind of mistake, she could not rely upon it happening. It was just not sensible to have the children in private schools when

there were free ones available. Somehow they had
started with the schools and worked back.

'There has to be a full term's notice,' said Sally.
'You're liable for fees for the next five months. That's
going to take what's owing up to about seven thousand. Look, don't worry. It's happening all the time.
People go bankrupt, husbands run off, someone falls
ill, dies. Children are forever being taken out of these
schools. There's nothing permanent about privilege.
That's its point, isn't it? It's the battle to stay on top.
All tooth and claw and you're forever fighting to keep
on your perch.'

'I hadn't thought about it like that,' said Natalie. It
seemed to her that whenever she asked a simple question she got a reproach in return.

'Now's your chance,' said Sally Bains. 'The compre-
hensives round here aren't bad. Of course they're on
strike a lot of the time. The Government means to
privatize all schools, in due course, but you might just
get a couple of years free schooling before the state
system collapses altogether from lack of funding.'

'I see,' said Natalie, unsure whether Sally Bains
approved or disapproved of free schools. Sally, of
course, had little emotional energy left over from her
marriage to approve or disapprove of anything. She
spoke out of the memory of herself as a political being,
young and vigorous, not as wife of Val Bains, unemployed back-sufferer and depressive.

'Ring up the headmaster of Quartermante. Don't let
them go to St John's. No one's got an O level out of
there for five years, and now it's GCSEs I don't think
they're even bothering to enter anyone: it's too
expensive. Still, it's a sort of free child minding service,
I suppose, even if it's not an education.'

What Sally could have told Natalie, as she had told

many another embarrassed parent in the past, was that all kinds of charities existed which would have been prepared, properly approached, to pay Ben and Alice's fees – the rich look after their own – and that representation to the board of governors might well have resulted in the waiving of the money owing. But she did not tell her; Natalie was too neat and too pretty and her husband had run off, and Sally could not help wishing, from time to time, that Val's back would improve sufficiently for him to be able to do what he kept threatening to do; look up the girl he had ditched in order to marry Sally and run off – with her. What Sally felt for Natalie, amazingly, was envy. But that's what being married to a depressive can do for a woman. How do I, Sonia, know all this? My husband Stephen, thank God, couldn't claim to be a depressive; he was an anal retentive paranoic, which is bad enough. And personally I border on the manic (out and out it pours, doesn't it, never stopping), but I reckon about two thirds of the women in the estate, all of us on the dole, were married to depressives at one time or another, or had our illegitimate children by them. And though we all started out as healthy, cheerful, female children, the male disease of depression is catching. Quite simply, the men pass it on to their womenfolk and, to use a dirty word, it's as fatal as AIDS. We drudge down to the post office to cash our drafts: we can't even get it together to have them paid direct into a bank.

My shrink – sorry, psychiatrist – says this is nonsense: women are depressives too, sit in hospital corridors, speechless and motionless, staring into space, just like men; unmarried ones too – but I reckon they caught it from their fathers.

Be that as it may, Sally failed to give Natalie proper sisterly help at a time when she needed it. Okay?

The Heart of the Country

In the meantime, Jax was restless at the end of his lead. He was hungry.

Natalie took the telephone number of the recommended school from Sally, and then its address. A phone call would cost ten pence and, if she was left waiting at the end of the line, possibly more. She would do better to call round in person. That would be free. Or would it? Perhaps the free schools, like the museums, would now charge her admission? A fee to see the headmaster?

Neatly dressed, clear-eyed little children with self-satisfied faces ran about the corridors as she left. That's what £1,250 a term can do for the young, here in the heart of the country.

Angus, driving past the school in the Audi Quattro, saw Natalie and Jax pass out through the school gates and pulled up beside them, with an enviable squealing of brakes, the kind that betokens a person of instant decision at the wheel. Natalie got in beside Angus. Jax, as if sensing the urgency of the situation, jumped into the back seat without demur. And on they all went towards Glastonbury.

'You again!' he said. 'Surprise, surprise!' He'd been up and down the road four times, waiting for her.

'I hope you don't mind dogs,' said Natalie. 'I hope he doesn't leave hairs on your nice new seats.'

'My wife will hoover them up,' said Angus. He was lying. 'And I don't mind anything so long as it's to do with you.'

He was getting fonder and fonder of Natalie by the minute. Female distress and incompetence, mixed with a soupçon of resistance, can do that to a man. Natalie wasn't looking her best that morning. She had forgotten her make-up, the walk to school had flattened her hair and she had holes in her tights. It reassured him: she looked altogether approachable.

'The truth of the matter is,' she said, 'I think my husband's left home.' She had to say it to someone. And so, at last, it became true.

She wouldn't go with Angus for a coffee. She said she had too much to do. He went all the way back to Waley and Rightly, estate agents, of which he was a director. Their offices nestled at the foot of Gurney Castle.

Cough, Cough, Wheeze, Gasp

Natalie went to the bank, to ask for a loan.

The bank manager, by name Jasper Jones, was a strikingly good-looking man in his early thirties, who would presently be moved to an urban branch and no doubt end up at Head Office. In the meantime he jogged along country lanes with as much confidence as if they had been city streets, dodging cow pats and slurry pools, knowing his life would not include them for ever. On a better day Natalie would have attempted to charm him, raising her dark-lashed blue eyes to his, and so forth, but not today.

'I would like to give you a loan, Mrs Harris,' he said, 'but there is no way I can, I'm afraid. If you came to me with any kind of security, or these days even without it but with some workable scheme for making money out of nothing, then of course I would look favourably upon a request to borrow. But just money out of the blue, for groceries? No. Social security does that kind of thing. I suggest you get down there before the office closes for lunch. Your house is not a security, as you may have thought, but a liability. There's an Inland Revenue bill outstanding: did you not know that? Of some forty thousand pounds – the tax people move fast. They can sell the house over your head, and at a lot less than market value, if they so choose.'

'They can't do that. I live there,' said Natalie. Now actually she was right, and she could have had a stop put on a compulsory sale through the courts, but who was there to tell her that? Not the bank manager. Harry had fraudulently built up an overdraft of eighteen thousand pounds, against a non-materializing million-pound order, and how else but by the rapid sale of the house was the bank manager to get his money back, after the Inland Revenue had taken their cut, and get to Head Office in the end. I am not saying this went through the front of Jasper Jones' mind, but it sure as hell passed somewhere through the back, enabling him to reply, firmly:

'They can and they do. They can sell everything except personal belongings, and I can assure you there's not much they see as personal, except a toothbrush or so. There is nothing wrong with accepting social security, Mrs Harris. A quarter of the country now depends on it, one way or the other. Just 30 per cent of the population works: the other 70 per cent live off their earnings.'

'But once you're on it,' asked Natalie, ever simple, 'how do you get off?'

'Ah!' said Jasper Jones. 'That's the problem. And by the way we don't encourage dogs in the bank. He seems very restless. Is he safe?'

'He's hungry,' said Natalie.

Natalie went to the DHSS offices and there saw one of their senior clerks, a single lady in her forties, who had gone straight from school into the social services and risen through the ranks by virtue of her competence and administrative abilities. Natalie could have described her by her rather heavy tweed suit and the long green scarf she wore knotted around her neck for warmth and shelter, but not by her face, which was unexceptional to the point of anonymity. She was professionally kind and considerate but felt, herself, that the sooner her clients (as she was now taught to call them) learned to stand on their own two feet, the better. Her name was Mary Alice Dodson, and I (Sonia) have crossed her path several times, one way or another. I hate her for her self-righteousness. Natalie didn't understand that she was hateful, and thought her perfectly pleasant. But then she saw herself as a supplicant, and not someone with rights. What a battle I was to have, raising Natalie's client-consciousness!

Mary Alice Dodson, having taken down a great deal of information about Natalie, said, in the kind of tone that can be construed as reproachful:

'So what it comes to is that you have no family you can turn to. Your children are without the normal aunts, uncles and grandparents. You're very much alone.'

'Yes.'

'There's no blame in it,' said Mary Alice, enigmatically, 'unless you're prepared to take it.'

I don't want to be unfair to Mary Alice. All women are our sisters. She went potholing in the Cheddar Gorge as a hobby. She is underpaid and overworked like anyone else and is a virgin at forty-three. Some women are (a few) and there's nothing wrong with that in itself. It's just that Mary Alice does seem to feel it's a woman's *fault* if she finds herself in the kind of emotional and/or practical quandaries which afflict women who insist on consorting with men, and bearing their children, in an area of high unemployment. If they'd only keep their bodies to themselves, Mary Alice thinks, how much more cheerful and decent a place the world would be. Mary Alice's hair is very coarse, straight and thick.

'Now your husband has left, you are not anticipating an alternative live-in relationship?'

'No. Are these questions necessary?' Natalie shouldn't have asked that.

'I have to ask these personal questions,' Mary Alice explained patiently to Natalie, 'only in order to establish some kind of background. If you register it as an abuse of privacy try to understand our position. There are more and more people out there trying to take unfair advantage of a system which is breaking down already.'

'I wouldn't ask for money if I didn't need it.'

'Nor would we offer it to you if you didn't,' said Mary Alice, sharply. She belongs underground in a cold, dark hole, and she knows it: she must, or else why does she go potholing?

'Of course', went on Mary Alice, 'there can be no question of the State subsidizing you yet. Your husband may turn up within the next week or so. I pass Dunbarton on my way to work in the morning. One of the more pleasant new bungalows around here. It must be worth quite a lot. Mortgaged?'

'I don't know.'

And do you know, Natalie didn't. 'My husband looks, looked after things like that,' she added, since Mary Alice looked so surprised, not even knowing it was a classic line, not even uttering a deprecatory little laugh at her own folly. Yes, really and truly, here she was at thirty-four and her husband had looked after all that. Or hadn't. Natalie had always thought the house moves had been from choice, not necessity. She had simply not understood her husband's nature. (And if you don't think this is likely consider all those women who live with bigamists, rapists, child molesters and such and never even guess.)

'Then you'd better find out before making any application to us. Of course, if you genuinely can't cope we will do the coping for you.'

'I just want to know my entitlements.'

'The Children's Officer will be up to see how the children are, that goes without saying.'

'The children? The children are fine.'

'I'm sure you think they are, but you must have had a shock, and may not be the person best fitted to tell. And, of course, as I say, your husband may be back.'

'I'm not sure I want him back,' said Natalie.

'If he can provide for you, the State won't have to. There might not be quite as much picking and choosing as you suppose.'

Down, down the hole, Mary Alice: into the black depths and may you get wedged, stuck tight, with your head in a cleft about to flood at any moment, and someone pulling at your legs and you just not budging. Down, into the icy torrent of your clients' despair.

'If I lose my home, will I be re-housed?' asked Natalie next. 'Will I get a council house?'

'It's not as easy as that. Too many women round here seem to think they only have to ask and it will be given. They even come in from outside the area, thinking they fancy a free view of the Tor and expecting us to play nanny. Are the children healthy?'

'Perfectly.'

'That's bad,' said Mary Alice. 'Or you might be able to notch up a housing point or two. Of course, we do have bed-and-breakfast accommodation for people who're evicted for no fault of their own, but there usually is fault. And there's an emergency hostel – but that's hardly for your class of person. You'd have to ask at Housing. But they're shut on Thursdays. They're in Shepton Mallet.'

'I don't think it will come to that,' said Natalie.

'You'd be surprised what things come to,' said Mary Alice. 'And, by the way, dogs are not allowed in these offices.'

Natalie went next to a solicitor, Alec Southey, and I'm not saying much about him, I'm sorry, because he was the one I, Sonia, went to about a parking ticket, whom I had an affair with, who wouldn't leave his wife, but on account of whom Stephen left me. He failed to tell Natalie about how she could have a stop put on the sale of the house: perhaps he just forgot but perhaps he was a friend of a) the Inland Revenue, b) the bank manager, c) Arthur, d) Angus; any of them or all of them would do. Alec was currently having an affair with the wife of a man away in Saudi Arabia a lot of the time, so not likely to *burst in*. I think Stephen bursting in on Alec and me made quite an impression – though, as it happens (I believe it often happens) it wasn't Alec Stephen hit and hated, it was me. Amazing how men stick together, even in these circumstances. Alec's tall, thin and dark. So are a lot of men. I keep thinking it's him I see across the street, and my heart stops, but it isn't him, after all. Can this be love? Anyway, now I'm inside this place there are no streets to see him across any more, only wards, and I don't seem to see him so often. Can this be sanity? Alec said to Natalie that dogs gave him asthma, and this at least I know to be true. Cough, cough, wheeze and gasp. Good!

Natalie then went off to see the police inspector, Jack Took, because Alec Southey said the police might well help her trace Harry, and she was shown into his office.

'I expect it's all a mistake,' said Natalie. 'I expect he'll turn up any minute. I expect he's lost his memory through stress. These things do happen.'

Jack Took, a kindly, twinkly fellow of the old school, said he expected that Harry Harris was at that very moment living it up on the Costa del Criminal with Miss Eddon Gurney 1978, using his credit cards to advantage, and possibly other people's as well. Had Natalie no idea of the kind of person she was married to?

'Apparently not,' said Natalie.

The police inspector talked about possible criminal proceedings against Harry; conduct which led to the closure of a factory and the throwing out of work of at least sixteen people, still with wages owing, was not just misrepresentation but downright fraud.

'I get the feeling you don't like my husband very much,' said Natalie, at which Jack Took threw back his head and laughed and laughed, so much and for so long he quite forgot to ask for a cup of tea for Natalie when his was brought in, but at least he didn't complain about the dog. He said he'd be in touch if anything transpired.

Love Your Enemy

Natalie went up and sat in the Abbey grounds. Now the Abbey, if you ask me, is a very masculine kind of place. If women have any place beneath the avenue of elegant ancient trees, it's scurrying here and there with dead hens to be plucked and fish to be gutted. The Abbots of Glastonbury were men of temporal power. They ruled the lands around, collected tithes, sold pardons, drained the Levels, grew rich and prosperous and excommunicated anyone who disagreed with them. Which last would cause about as much distress, I suppose, as depriving someone of their colour TV today. William the Conqueror lined abbots and monks up against a wall, killed the lot (by way of bow and arrow, I presume) and replaced them with their Norman equivalents. Later, Henry VIII did much the same: chopped off the Abbot's head on top of the Tor and replaced him. Later still Cromwell evicted the lot and hacked down much of the fabric of the Cathedral. I am not surprised that Natalie felt no sense of comfort or support emanating from the site of the high altar, or indeed from the bleak oblong of Arthur's grave.

'All day long the noise of battle rolled' writes the poet of these sacred places. Fight, bash, hack, pierce, behead, crush – all in the service of God – what a record these religious folk have that we're expected to take so seriously! Natalie would have felt healthier vibes in the local supermarket. Or indeed down in the dry-cleaners where I, Sonia, used to spend quite a lot of my days in Glastonbury – waiting for the school bell to ring and my duties as unpaid childminder for the State to resume. I like the dry-cleaners. I like the sense of refreshment and renewal. I like the way dirty old torn clothes are dumped, to be returned clean and wholesome in their slippery transparent cases. Better than confession any day. Here there is a true sense of rebirth, redemption, salvation. What was old and horrid will do you for a day or so more, my dear, now Westaways the cleaners have blessed it! I would try to tell all this to Jeanette, the high priestess who ran the dry-cleaners, but it made her embarrassed. She thought I talked too much, and she was right. But there is always so much to be said, and so seldom anyone to tell it to. I made a fool of myself down in the dry-cleaners, I suppose: showing need. You have to be careful in this life: you shouldn't show need, or you'll be despised. Look what happened when I begged and pleaded with Stephen to stay with me and the children.

'I love you,' I said. 'I need you. Please don't abandon us.'

'Love!' he sneered. 'You don't even know the meaning of the word. I expect you used it often enough to Alec – and took him in for a time.'

'You can't just throw away a marriage like this!'

'It's you who've thrown it away.' And how could I deny it? I had spoiled everything good and valuable between us. 'But this is our home – you can't sell it!'

The marital home (as it came to be known) was a farmhouse; warm, untidy, cosy. I'd made the garden beautiful. I hadn't had time to do much to the interior.

'I can do what I like,' he said. 'And will. As for calling it a home – it's a mess. You're a slut as well as a whore.'

Well, he was angry, and very upset, and right to be. I had done wrong.

'I have three children under five and it's exhausting,' I defended myself.

'Not so exhausting you can't sneak out to your lover,' he said. 'You're filthy: like an animal! I wonder how many of those children are mine?'

There seemed no explaining to him how weak the sexual charge was between me and Alec: how that was not what it was about at all. An affair that went on three long summer months – and we only went to bed (well, not bed, actually in the back of the car) four times, and then it seemed accidental, even rather embarrassing, what did that amount to? We preferred holding hands and sighing; he wanted to know what was going on in my head, and that seemed to me totally entrancing: and he no doubt just enjoyed the romantic intensity of it all. Life is so short, isn't it? I didn't register my behaviour as infidelity at the time; though in retrospect I can see how I hurt and humiliated Stephen. Anyway, the more I wept and pleaded and cut my wrists, the more determined he was to leave.

Of course, it did later transpire (after the divorce, after the selling of the home, after he somehow managed to be living very comfortably at the other end of the country, and with one of my girlfriends, what's more – and I was stuck up at 19 Wendover, Boxover, living with the kids on social security – he having argued in court that they weren't his) that he'd been having affairs throughout the course of the marriage. He'd decided, long before the arrival of Alec, that he wanted out, and had waited for the excuse to come along whereby we could be divorced, and I would take the moral blame. And of course I took it; I lapped it up. Ever heard a man say 'It was my fault the marriage broke up'? No. Those are women's lines. They'll stare at you with their black eyes and broken noses and say,

'My fault! I provoked him.' Sometimes I despair. And I'm no better than anyone. Looking back over these pages, I see I've been apologizing for having hurt and humiliated a man who pretended love, felt none, and did me a great deal of damage.

I wonder if my shrink (sorry, psychiatrist) was a woman not a man I'd be in a better or a worse state, after three months in this place? Probably better, but I wouldn't be having so nervy and enjoyable a time, would I?

I pleaded insane at my trial, though I didn't think at the time that I actually was. Now I'm not so sure. Perhaps the first step to sanity is knowing you're insane? Round and round we go, though the monsters do seem to have taken up positions quite far back inside my head. They still stare with baleful eyes, but at least they're not clawing or rending. Enough.

Now where did we leave Natalie? Ah yes. Sitting on the bench in the grounds of the ruined Glastonbury Abbey, having joined the ranks of the supplicants and dispossessed, and wearing quite the wrong shoes for it: they had peep-toes and high heels, as worn by those who think life is for the enjoying, not the mere getting through. Jax sat at her side; but he twitched rather, and looked haunted, as if he too were wondering where his next meal was coming from.

Now two people came walking towards her. One was the groundsman, Peter Ferris by name, the other a Japanese tourist who was engaging him in conversation. Peter had a beard and Jesus-eyes, and was referred to by the local children as a hippie. But then they'd call anyone a hippie who, if a woman, wore skirts longer than mid-calf, and, if a man, wore an earring. Peter Ferris was explaining to the Japanese tourist, a small, elegant man in a smart grey suit, who looked as if he believed the world was real, not an illusion, about the Glastonbury Thorn. How Jesus had come to Glastonbury in the year AD 11 with his uncle Joseph of Aramathea, a tin trader. Glastonbury at that time was an island. Jesus had blessed the thorn tree, which had bloomed on Christmas Day ever since.

'You've *seen* it bloom on Christmas Day?'

'I have,' said Peter, failing to add that this particular type of thorn is winter flowering, that is to say between November and January, a sad, battered bloom or so appears. If you ask me, Jesus didn't bless it at all, he cursed it as he did the fig tree (I have felt protective towards that fig tree, poor barren thing, ever since I was sterilized). Christianity really is a man's religion: there's not much in it for women except docility, obedience, who-sweeps-a-room-as-for-thy-cause, downcast eyes and death in childbirth. For the men it's better: all power and money and fine robes, the burning of heretics – fun, fun, fun! – and the Inquisition fulminating from the pulpit.

The Japanese tourist went away to explore the Monks' Kitchen and Peter the groundsman sat down next to Natalie and Jax. He carried a pointed stick, the better to spear and dispose of the litter the tourists left.

'You know you're not supposed to have dogs up here?' he asked.

She hadn't known. He said he didn't suppose it mattered much.

'Fine beast,' he said.

'He's upset,' she said.

'Why's that?'

'His master's gone away.'

'Bad luck,' said Peter.

'What is more,' she said, 'he's hungry.'

'Then feed him.'

'I haven't any money.'

'Then give him away,' said Peter, grandly, as if amiable recipients of large dogs littered every corner of his grounds. And so of course they did, in essence. Prick, with Peter's pointed stick at a piece of rubbish: pick it up and prick again, and lo, all is tidiness and order, and there's another canine housed, and the can of dog food whirring happily round in an electric can-opener, and the hungry looking up, and being fed. All things are possible.

'How? Where?' she asked. These were the questions she had been asking all day, but no one seemed to answer. 'Why?' she was leaving till later.

'Go where the food is,' he said, and stood up – or unfolded, for he was remarkably tall and thin – and smiled. 'The general rule is, if you have to live off crumbs, make sure they fall from a rich man's table. They're more plentiful.' And of course he was right: the poor man in Frankfurt is better off than the poor man in Addis Ababa. The problem is finding the air fare from one place to another.

Where the food is, at least locally, was of course The Tessen, the delicatessen where Gerard gloomed and Pauline tried to cheer him up.

'Cash flow,' Gerard mourned, putting out trays of preservative-free sausages – always a problem. After three days they smelt high and the customers started complaining, and after four days those unsold simply had to be thrown out. 'You could live a whole life in the old days and never ever hear about cash flow. We used to call it bloody debt. We should never have been conned into starting this mad enterprise. It goes against every principle I ever had. But you insisted, and now look!'

'It takes time for new businesses to break even,' said

Pauline. Four whole years, they said, at the New Business Studies Course she attended, and she could see it might well be true, if Gerard insisted on buying and throwing out preservative-free sausages. She knew of a new brand of excellent, reasonably priced, spicy sausages which the customers would appreciate, containing only the least harmful of available preservatives, with a high profit margin and a good shelf life, but Gerard would not hear of it. He would do things the hard and honourable way, and the shop would stay half empty, and such customers as there were would feel nervous at spending their money on luxuries, as Gerard sliced the salmon with socialist reluctance. (Don't get me wrong, Sonia is a socialist through and through. It's just some socialists are on the dour side when it comes to spending money.)

'I suppose you learned that in adult education.' Gerard had declined to attend the course. He said business was a matter of common sense.

'I did.'

'Small businesses!' he mourned. 'This is a shop, not a small business. This Government is trying to turn us into a Far Eastern nation, with everyone living off everyone else's scraps.'

Sonia knows that, Pauline knows that, everyone knows that; why does Gerard have to go on about it all the time? You may have got the notion that Sonia doesn't much care for Gerard. Too right she doesn't. Poncey little creep. But the shrink doesn't like to hear that kind of talk. For poncey little creep read modern-day Samuel Smiles. Gerard had been going on all morning about the way Pauline had failed to collect a cheque from Natalie, and Pauline, after the manner of wives, instead of telling him to go fuck himself, was saying, sorry, sorry, sorry.

'Talk of the devil,' he said, and there was Natalie looking in the window of The Tessen, hesitant. Jax, on a lead, was with her.

'She'd better not bring that dog in here,' said Gerard. 'We try to keep this place hygienic.'

'She might be coming in with a cheque,' offered Pauline, but she didn't really think so. Tales of the collapse of Harrix and the Harris' marriage had come to her from all sides. She hadn't liked to pass the news on to Gerard or no doubt he'd be crosser than ever about the way she, Pauline, had let Natalie run up the account. Natalie pushed open the door and came in with Jax. Pauline thought she'd better get in before Gerard did.

'I'm sorry,' she said, 'no dogs in the shop.'

But Jax was already in, staring up at Gerard as he cut chunks of Brie and caper, pre-wrapped to meet the rush (what rush?) and all cut at 6 ounces, that is to say, too small for the generously minded, and too large for the economical. Just wrong. Gerard stopped wrapping and stared back at Jax. It was love at first sight. These things happen. Jax, not to put too fine a point on it, smiled back. Some dogs can, and do.

'What I wondered was,' said Natalie, 'if you would take the dog in payment of my account. He is valuable. He's got a pedigree.' It seemed, to Natalie, a fair exchange. Dog owners always overrate the value of their pet to others, and Natalie was no exception.

Pauline waited for Gerard to speak, and Gerard for Pauline to speak, so Natalie spoke again, into the silence.

'I can't afford to feed him,' said Natalie. 'It's silly to go on trying.'

Gerard said, surprisingly, 'Your children won't like

81

it. Children think, if you can give dogs away, you can give them away.'

Pauline said, 'How do you know a thing like that, Gerard? We've never had any children.'

Gerard said, 'But I was a child myself. You forget that.'

'It's years since we had a dog,' said Pauline, who couldn't remember her own childhood and so could scarcely be expected to remember his.

'He's a splendid animal,' said Gerard.

They were hooked. They were giving up the expected years of freedom: throwing away all they had gained by the non-having of children – look – suddenly – a pet! Madness!

'He'll eat up all the profit,' said Pauline.

'He eats anything,' said Natalie.

'Dogs shouldn't eat just anything,' said Gerard, severely. 'They should eat a properly balanced diet.'

'He could eat what we throw out,' said Pauline. 'Such as sausages, old quiche.'

'He certainly can't,' said Gerard. 'Far too much fat in sausages.'

'So you'll have him?' asked Natalie.

'Of course we'll have him,' said Gerard. 'Tell the children he's on loan. They can come and see him when they want. How much do you think he's worth?'

'A hundred and fifty,' said Natalie, vaguely.

'Your account is a hundred and forty-five,' said Gerard, 'approximately.'

He took five pounds from the till and handed it to Natalie. Pauline gaped. Natalie did not refuse it, and left without Jax, feeling some predestined event had been properly and ritually accomplished. She found she did not miss Jax any more than she missed Harry, and concluded that missing people and animals was a luxury that could perhaps be afforded later, but not now.

The Tessen filled up with customers as soon as Natalie had gone: the till pinged merrily. Even the 6 oz packets of Brie with capers sold, and Gerard got rid of three whole rounds for someone's impromptu office party. Pauline patted Jax and Gerard said:

'Do remember hygiene! Always wash your hands after handling an animal.' But he said it amiably and even smiled at a customer and Pauline had the feeling that the shop would do better henceforth. She extracted the additive-free sausages, already rather high, from the cold shelf, and fed them secretly to Jax, who ate heartily and gratefully. She was glad to know he was not fussy.

Peter told Natalie to go where the food was, and she did, and it just happened to work out all right. Or so Natalie says. I, Sonia, think it was more than that. It took courage on Natalie's part to walk down Debtor's Row and into the shop, and outface her own humiliation. She did it for Jax's sake, not her own. Of course it turned out well. Unlike virtue, courage is not its own reward. It has results.

Justifications

I had better tell you more about the Bridgewater carnival. For one week every year, around the time of Guy Fawkes Day (that is to say at the beginning of November, when the pagans traditionally held their fire-and-rebirth ceremonies, and committed their grudge burnings and their human sacrifices) the carnival clubs, which have been secretly active all year, unveil their floats, and parade them in procession down the misty streets of small West Country towns, lights flaring and music blaring. They come a hundred strong, and each float can be as many feet long, and every one has perhaps ten, twenty, fifty souls on board, dressed as the theme of the float suggests, whether it be 'Winter Wonderland' (ice crystals), 'Revenge of the Khan' (warlords) or 'Denizens of the Deep' (Father Neptune's slaves) or such. These glittery creatures parade or dance beneath the hot light-bulbed roofs, or pose, if a tableau is required, in frozen immobility in the icy November wind. Each float is pulled by a tractor (or two or three if it's what you might call a major entry) and followed up by a generator (or two or three). Crowds fill the roads, charity boxes rattle, children skitter between hot-dog stands and the vendors of strange flat silvery balloons and translucent Force-Be-With-You wands, and the elderly pull their hats over their ears against the cold. Marshals push back the spectators as the first police cars appear, and the ambulance, and the noise of the leading girls' band drifts in the wind and the first great unwieldy, noisy, brilliant box of delights eases round the corner and the carnival is here! There are no cheers from the crowd as it passes, dancing or singing, or other demonstrations of good cheer: this is not a participation show. No. It is a religious ceremony: applause when it comes is scattered and reverential. Those who live in the heart of the country are not swift or noisy in their enthusiasm. Feelings, nevertheless, run high, don't think they don't! Fights break out, strong words are spoken, a strange still drink is consumed – the local cider. It rots the brain cells quicker than any other form of alcohol, they say, and only 20p the pint.

It is against the carnival rules for commercial firms to enter floats, but of course they do. How can you not let the local tractor dealer have an advertising float, when you're using his entire range of second-hand tractors to pull the collecting floats? For all this, allegedly, is in aid of charity. People throw money: even the meanest. People can't just enjoy themselves, can they! They have to have an excuse.

Why am I describing all this? Because last year someone burned to death on the WAEADA float, and I it was (well, and Ros) who set the float on fire, and I am trying to feel remorse in order to get out of here. So I have to set up the background properly. 'Here' is the Eddon Hill Psychiatric Hospital. My psychiatrist's name is Bill Mempton, Dr Bill Mempton, and at the moment I have a positive transference towards him which means that if he doesn't shave I think he looks rather good, and if he's late I worry in case he's done himself in. This latter is not an insane worry: quite a few psychiatrists at this hospital have killed themselves by what has become known as the Eddon Method: that is to say, in the home garage, engine running, hose pipe from the exhaust to the window crack, to be found by the spouse and/or children. They have even managed to out-suicide their own patients. Since there are 30 psychiatrists and 1,200 patients, and the latter are watched in case they do escape this jolly old world, I think that is a pretty appalling statistic. Something like 10 per cent of psychiatrists committing *felo de se* to only .005 per cent of patients. Who needs watching most? I ask myself. Since the patients are insane and the psychiatrists are sane (I am not arguing this point: few of the latter bark like dogs or chew their underlips away altogether) I think what the dead are trying to tell us is that to stay alive is insane when death is available.

Bill (how cosy! how almost intimate we have become) gets furious when I make this point, talks about the low wages, high stress, falling status, family difficulties and so forth endured by medics in the psychiatric branch of the profession. All I reply is if you can't stand the patients, stay out of the ward! You do them no good by knocking yourself off in this way. What sort of example etc., etc.

You see? I can heap coals of fire on psychiatrists' heads, but not do the reverse: can't allow them to heap coals on mine. Murder of the self seems to be reprehensible and disgraceful; the man – or woman – slaughter of another as the high point of a carnival quite another matter – merely the final event of an ancient ritual, consciously or unconsciously consented to by the victim.

86

Living Rough

Well, at least I never had to live rough, as did Flora, Natalie's cleaning girl. Her address was The Caravan, The Rubbish Dump, Eddon Gurney, where the crows wheeled and the flies swarmed. She lived there with her boyfriend Bernard. They'd spend the cold weather in the caravan's double bunk, and so didn't really suffer, as others would, during the winters. But the old felt the cold that year; they had no love to keep them warm; they died like flies of hypothermia. It was in all the papers. Flora's mother was fifty-three. That to Flora seemed old. When the temperature fell below freezing she would ring her mother in her council flat in Leeds to see how she was. She didn't put money in the box. She used Harry Harris' phonecard, which she'd nicked. At least she had a mother. My mother had a continental background, and was never very healthy (the war, I suppose) and died when I was three. My father was a journalist and drifted off into nowhere: he was an alcoholic, more or less; well, as I say, he was a journalist. I was a bright child; got a degree in Eng. Lit., married Stephen, a West Country engineer, and thought, all that is behind me. My mother, my mother's terrible memories: my father, my father's weakness. Stephen and I will be happy for ever in the heart of the country. We will start from here on down. That's what I thought.

Dr Bill Mempton asked me today why I identified so with Flora? Flora, who sat on that float as Mrs House-wife Princess 1986. Talk about false pretences! Flora, who lived in sin, with Bernard? No Mrs, she! House-wife? The nearest Flora ever got to housewifery was sloshing a too-wet mop over Natalie's floor! But never you mind details like that. This is the heart of the country. Flora was the prettiest and youngest of us, and Angus and Arthur wanted her to be Mrs Housewife Princess, so she got to sit in the gold conch shell at the carnival, as half-Madonna, half-Virgin. Both the mother who loves her child, and the girl who looks forward to love.

What I did inherit from my mother, who as a young girl was in Dachau, is the vision of the charnel house inside my head, the spitting devils and the piles of dead human flesh. It's a race memory, that's all. Nothing important. Nothing, good Dr Bill Mempton, that you should have to fear.

Bargains

This is how Arthur first encountered Flora. Picture her
a week or so after Harry Harris had left Natalie. Natalie
had failed to turn up at Arthur's antique shop on a
Tuesday and a Thursday and a Tuesday again; and
Arthur reckoned that was about that, and didn't want
things stirred up anyway because an affair with a
securely married woman is one thing, if you are
securely married yourself, and an affair with a woman
whose husband has left her is quite another. But he
missed her: he was partly grateful she hadn't seen fit to
make emotional demands on him and partly aggrieved.

Arthur went up to the tip one Friday morning, after
a restless night, to see if anything had turned up. Now
well-established antique dealers such as Arthur don't
regularly visit local rubbish tips. They leave that to the
runners, knockers and totters, those scurrying people
at the bottom of the trader's pile, those whose function
it is to locate, recognize and rescue the scraps and
remnants the past has left behind, anything from a
broken leg by Chippendale to a farmer's pig bench to
a piece of cracked Lalique to an old postcard. Some of
it – not much, but some – does escape their searching
fingers, their greedy eyes, and ends up on the local
rubbish dump, tipped there by the innocent, those who
think an old fireplace is better ripped out and replaced
by a modern one, and that flat doors are preferable
to panelled ones; indeed that anything new must be
preferred to something old. And though it was not
any more Arthur's role in the complex structure of the

antique trade – he who had risen to have his own shop, and actually sell to the private punters, and not just to others within the trade – to go scavenging, but to leave all that to those whose business it properly was, he sometimes did. He stopped the Citroën by the tip in the early morning, and took a stroll, just to see what was in there. He couldn't help it. He loved the excitement.

This morning he was surprised to see a caravan parked some little distance from the row of skips where the public came to dump their black bags of peelings, eggshells and cat hairs, their old fridges, shoes, bottles and occasionally their rather good sidetables, not to mention their deceased grandma's bentwood rocking chair. The semi-official totter at the Eddon Gurney tip was a certain Hopalong, recently taken into hospital, as Arthur knew well enough.

The caravan had, as it were, its back to the tip. It looked up towards the cliff, quarried unnaturally out of the hillside some twenty years back, and now awash with creepers and flowers. A pretty enough place, if you didn't look back over your shoulder, and held your nose in high summer. Just now, in the spring, it was at its best.

A young man came sauntering round the side of the caravan. He had cropped blonde hair, brushed upwards – the modern style – wide eyes, and a chiselled, handsome, rather cold face; he wore tight jeans and a T-shirt and was pulling on a leather jacket with many zips. He seemed aggressive. He walked towards Arthur and didn't stop walking, or talking. 'Any old iron, any old iron!' he jeered. 'Any old Georgian chairs, any old stripped pine washstands, left over from last year's November 5th? No, buster, is the answer: no straight off. If there's anything going, I get it, and you and your sort are not welcome up here.'

'What makes you think I'm a dealer?' asked Arthur.

'I can tell them from a mile off,' said Bernard. 'Scum of the earth.'

At that moment, as Arthur stood his ground – he was not a coward and had his dignity to think about – Flora came out of the caravan. She was wrapped in a silk kimono and her hair was dishevelled. She seemed to Arthur entirely beautiful – the Virgin and the Madonna mixed in one – as young, bright and careless as the flowers which draped the cliff behind her, and with entirely the wrong man, that is to say Bernard of the many zips and uncouth attitude. Bernard turned to see what Arthur was gawping at and saw Flora.

'Get the coffee on, Flora, for God's sake,' Bernard said. 'Stop trolling about not properly dressed.' She went back inside, giggling, but not without a flash of bare white breast beneath black and red silk. As I say, Arthur was a fine figure of a man, and beneath the leather Bernard could seem quite weedy.

'I don't want to tread on any toes,' said Arthur, mildly enough. 'I was expecting to see Hopalong.'

'I live here now,' said Bernard. 'I know you! You're the geezer up at Castle Antiques. You're the feller having the affair with my old lady's employer. Hopalong said you sometimes came up.'

'You can't have a caravan up here,' said Arthur, 'it's illegal. And you can't make insinuations like that, without finding a knife between your ribs one of these dark nights.'

'We're all illegal these days,' said Bernard. 'Even the police, and it wasn't so much an insinuation as a congratulation.'

'In that case you'd better come up and see me some

time,' said Arthur. Totters need dealers and dealers need totters in the same way as bread needs cheese and vice versa. It is better for the cheddar not to quarrel with the slice.

Arthur looked over Bernard's shoulder and saw the source of Bernard's temporary unwisdom, a rather good Georgian chair on top of the skip marked 'cardboard only' in Hopalong's crabby hand. Poor Hopalong, dead a day, and already someone filling his shoes! But there's a good living in totting: it was bound to happen.

'Let me know how it goes,' he said.

'I have my own contacts,' said Bernard.

'I doubt that,' said Arthur, and drove off.

'You shouldn't have said that about him and Natalie Harris,' said Flora, back in the caravan, taking off the kimono. 'It was only I saw her go in there one Tuesday.'

'Hit the nail on the button, if you ask me,' said Bernard. 'Good to know the wrinklies are still at it. There's hope for us yet.'

'That's where you're wrong,' said Flora.

The general hopelessness of their lot was Bernard and Flora's theme song. They sang it happily as the sun rose and the sun set. Even when they were both working, him on a tractor or down the school gate selling smack (only once: he got frightened), she up at the Harrises or doing school dinners (only for a week: she couldn't stand the grease and heat), they saw themselves as irrevocably and permanently unemployed. They had their little home and it was knee-deep in flowers. It was better than a cottage any day because all you had to do was move it an inch here or an inch there and you didn't have to pay rates. They got by; they had each other: they got by very nicely.

There was a screech of Citroën brakes. Better to make

92

friends than enemies. Besides, he wanted another glimpse of Flora.

'Would you like a job?' Arthur asked Bernard, who appeared naked in the caravan door.

'Who, me? I've got a job. I'm totting.'

'Totting's part time. This is a proper job.'

'What sort of proper job?'

'Down Avon Farmers. New trading company. A hundred and twenty a week.'

'What's the catch?'

'Hard work,' said Arthur. 'Long hours. Holding your tongue and minding your own business.'

'Make it a hundred and fifty,' said Bernard.

'A hundred and thirty,' said Arthur, 'and I don't know why I bother.' But a sharp bright boy was needed up at Avon Farmers and Arthur knew a sharp bright boy when he saw one. Nor did he want too many insinuations, let alone congratulations, floating around the countryside. He had his wife to think about.

'Perhaps you'll bring up that chair some time,' said Arthur. 'Bit of old rubbish but might be worth something.'

'I will,' said Bernard.

And that's how Bernard got the job at Avon Farmers – where presently he was to meet up with Natalie – by knowing too much and speaking his mind.

Arthur drove on to meet Angus, who was looking over the new Avon Farmers Trading Estate. This consisted of a corrugated iron barn and a group of Portakabins at the end of a farm track, to the north of Glastonbury Tor. Here Avon Farmers – a nebulous grouping of farmers, farm suppliers and businessmen – were to sell cheap imported agricultural chemicals and foodstuffs. By the time the Ministry inspectors got to hear of the existence of the warehouse, it would have evaporated, or, if it proved very successful, have moved on to the next county. Such subterfuge would not have been necessary had unreasonable EEC regulations not prevented the sale of certain fertilizers, growth promoters, hormones, insecticides and fungicides – used to advantage and without harming a soul in various parts of the world – to the detriment of British farmers. As it was, the home producers deserved the best deal they could get, and Avon Farmers meant to see they got it.

'Time you got a new car, Arthur,' said Angus, speaking from his Quattro.

'I'm fond of the old Citroën,' said Arthur. 'They don't make cars like this any more. I've found us a new lad. Lives up at the tip in a caravan with the most beautiful girl in the world.'

'Who? Not Natalie Harris?'

'Not Natalie,' said Arthur, severely.

'Lucky she's got you to lean on,' said Angus. 'In this the hour of her distress.'

'Me?' said Arthur, surprised.

'So they say,' said Angus.

'Not any more,' said Arthur. 'She's gone right off me.'

'I'm glad to hear that,' said Angus. 'I wouldn't want to tread on your toes.'

'Wouldn't you? Why not?'

'There's a rather good piece coming up in Friday's auction, Arthur. I'd appreciate your holding back.'

'Say no more. 'Tis done. What?'

'A davenport. Original Waring and Gillow. Just for a friend. A personal favour. A sprat to catch a mackerel.'

'Any friend of yours is a friend of mine, Angus, and your sprats are other people's mackerels. How's the Quattro?'

'Fantastic! How's the Citroën? Really? Sounds a bit clanky, to me.'

'It's like the wife,' said Arthur. 'Wearing out, but I'm fond of her.'

The wind was chilly. A too wide, bonded lorry crept up a too narrow lane towards them.

'What's that?'

'The stuff from Brazil, with any luck,' said Angus. 'Now we can really get going.'

'I suppose it's safe,' said Arthur.

'Good God,' said Angus, 'don't be such an old woman. DDT did us fine for decades. It doesn't change overnight. But look at the fuss they make now!'

'Give my love to Natalie when you see her,' said Arthur.

'I certainly will,' said Angus.

Well, a nod is as good as a wink to a county auctioneer, and so Natalie was sold to Angus against a return unspecified, but one day to be claimed. So the world proceeds, by one good turn, balanced by another. And the local insects bit the dust and calves and piglets got a load of growth promoters which fed carcinogens into the food chain, but who were they to care? They were too busy balancing their sudden, new, startling weight on the already too flimsy slats in the intensive care unit. And their owners got richer by the good, lean, popular kilo.

Redemption

When I try to write about Flora I keep wandering off
into the villainy of men. The point is that pretty young
women are expendable. Nobody likes them, except the
men who are currently involved with them. Their
mothers envy them, their fathers are disturbed by
them, their plainer siblings resent them, their teachers
dislike them. They have a hard time growing up, and
a hard time when grown. A pretty girl driving a Mini
will be driven off the road by lorry drivers as a matter
of course. What's she doing on the road? Driving is
work, not entertainment. Professors refuse to give them
degrees, in case they're accused of prejudice. Their
husbands don't trust them. Everyone knows what a
pretty girl is *for*, that's the trouble. If Flora had been
plainer, Bernard might have married her and not
treated her like a skivvy and a slave. (Plain girls marry
earlier, statistically, than pretty ones.) Look at her now,
as I do, cleaning Natalie's floor long after Natalie had
the wherewithal to pay her for so doing. Pretty, and
therefore persecuted! Flora's piled-up, streaked-in, friz-
zed-out hair has toppled halfway down her creamy
cheek. She keeps trying to push it up again with her
delicate white fingers, and has put a streak of grime
across that selfsame creamy cheek. This is, I admit,
beginning to get to me. How sad that these things must
pass! The creamy cheek one day will be no longer; as
will that female movement of the hands through the
hair, to puff and prettify. Sad, I say – yet that part of
me given over to jealousy and envy is not sorry, but

glad, that all things flesh are mortal, especially the flesh of the prettier members of the great universal sisterhood.

'I'm not going to work here for nothing,' said Flora, crossly, putting away the mop, helping Natalie extract Angus' dead hen, feathers and all, from the freezer. 'Why should I wash your floors, if not for money? Bernard says if you like he'll come and take away a couple of chairs in lieu.'

'Those chairs cost eighty-five pounds each two months ago. I only owe you fifteen pounds.'

'You should have bought antiques,' said Flora. 'Then they'd have had a re-sale value.'

'Harry liked new things,' said Natalie. These days she talked about Harry whenever she could. She thought she should. He'd been gone for three weeks. She had told the children he'd gone to Spain on business, and that there was trouble getting money through. That's why Ben wouldn't have a new briefcase for his books and Alice six new hair slides. She thought Alice believed her but that Ben did not. She'd told them they were changing schools at half term and Alice had turned white and said nothing and Ben had flushed and thrown a book at her and said he hated her.

'Always a mistake to do what a man likes,' said Flora now, as if she knew everything in the world. 'They get bored, if they have everything their own way.'

'So it seems,' said Natalie. Why was she confiding in the help? She regretted it, now.

'And he just walked out without a word!' said Flora. She felt like Natalie's younger sister, which was why she kept coming up to Dunbarton and working for no money. 'Aren't men pigs. But I can't believe you didn't see it coming.'

'If I was someone different I expect I would have,' Natalie said. 'But I'm me.'

'You don't do much screaming or shouting,' said Flora.

'There's no one to hear me,' said Natalie, sadly, and apart from Flora, there was indeed no one. Only Angus, who had asked himself to dinner, out of the blue, to eat his chicken. It proved impossible to pluck the feathers from a deep-frozen hen, but Flora offered to at least hack off the head with a chopper before she left.

'You won't have the nerve, Mrs Harris,' she said and Natalie accepted the offer with relief. She had only ever bought oven-ready birds.

The heavy knife whacked down upon the creature's neck, stretched as it was across the chopping board, head dangling, and a frozen globule of blood flew across the room and landed upon the print of Van Gogh's sunflowers.

'I never liked that picture,' said Natalie. 'Although I know I'm supposed to. Could I ask you something, Flora?'

'Ask away.'

'Did you steal my jewellery?'

'No.'

'Then he did it,' said Natalie. 'The bastard,' and she picked up a cup and threw that at the sunflowers. The cup broke and the picture fell off the wall. The return of rage, as I say, marks the beginning of recovery. It was at that point that Natalie stopped walking round like a zombie and thereafter flustered and wept and stormed and went round with red eyes and a haggard face like any other wife left suddenly with no money and the children. It takes years to recover properly, of course, before you can assume that because you woke bright eyed and calm to the day, you will continue thus until its end, without suffering a fit of melancholy, rage, distress, remorse, jealousy or some other unpleasant emotion. One in every three marriages ends in divorce. It happened to Natalie, it happened to me, it had happened to most of us on the carnival float that night – and all agree, all we have in the end are our friends.

The hen lay divided, gently thawing. Disgusting, really, the way people eat animals. I can never work out what stops them from eating each other. It would save so much trouble and hassle, and would efficiently recycle essential nutrients. Our agricultural land would be allowed to restore itself, and cease being the mere dull base for chemical fertilizers on which our crops are grown. For that is what the English soil has become. This whim – and it is nothing more – which obsesses humankind, that it is morally allowed to mass-produce animals in order to devour them, but morally disallowed to eat its own dead, will be the end of us.

Be all that as it may, saner, nicer and less cannibalistic people than me began to turn their heads to the sun the day Natalie threw a cup at Van Gogh's sunflowers.

Improvement

Sally went home from work, expecting to open her front door and see, as usual, Val in his armchair staring into space, with an assortment of pills and ointments beside him, the television not even on and the *Guardian* flung into a corner in disgust. But that day she opened her front door and found her husband up a ladder re-pasting wallpaper; the fire was burning, the windows were open and there were no pills in sight. When she came into the room, Val got down off the ladder, crossed to her, pecked her cheek, and relieved her of her shopping and took it into the kitchen. 'What happened?' she asked.

'The pain went,' he said. 'I think my Mars passed out of opposition to my Jupiter.'

'I don't understand that,' she said.

'We were mad enough to move to the West Country,' he said, 'instead of somewhere rational, so what's the point of fighting. We'll live as the natives do. We'll believe in astrology and I'll join Scientists Against the Bomb and have a CND sticker on the car.'

'There's a laser printing firm starting up in Street,' said Sally. 'One of the parents told me. You could try there for a job.'

She shouldn't have pushed her luck; she knew as soon as she'd spoken. (You have to watch your words, if you're living with a depressive.) But Val didn't react badly at all.

'I might well do that,' was all he said. 'Find out the address, will you?'

And as for Pauline and Gerard, they had their best day ever in The Tessen and, after closing up, took Jax out for a walk, as had become their custom.

'I still think bread at 90p the loaf is outrageous,' said Gerard. 'But I suppose if people want to buy it one shouldn't stop them.'

Jax nosed and snuffed amongst spring grasses. Rain had been falling: the sun suddenly slanted from the west, out from under a line of heavy grey clouds onto wet new foliage, and everything was brilliantly, almost unbearably, acid green: the colour quivered all around for five minutes or so, subduing even Jax so that he returned to trot at their heels.

'Growing old doesn't matter,' said Pauline. 'Not even growing old and childless. All this remains. We're just part of it: a product of it.'

Her husband tucked his arm in hers, without comment, and presently the colour scale returned to normal, and Jax took off again. Sometimes in the evening he would look melancholy and stare reproachfully at his new owners, and turn his head away even from Good Boy chocolate drops, and then they imagined he was missing the Harris household, but for the most part he was lively, cheerful and rewarding. Pauline fed him with high sausages and ham scraps when Gerard wasn't looking: and Gerard the same, when Pauline wasn't. Since Jax tended to be, if anything, underfed in their anxiety for his health, he did very well by these furtive arrangements.

Bernard and Flora had carved a fireplace into the cliff; Bernard had set up a clean, empty oil drum nearby and spent a morning filling it with water, so now they had a constant water supply. Their privy was the nearby quarry: they heaped leaves to make things decent, but used other people's water closets in the towns and villages when they could. Birds sang, grass swayed and flowers glowed. It was as near paradise, Bernard and Flora thought, as could be achieved, there on the edge of the council rubbish tip. They were not lonely – there was a constant to-ing and fro-ing in the near distance, as cyclists rode up to deposit single wine bottles, or men on trucks dumped industrial waste (forbidden) – yet still they were private. Mostly those who visited the tip were householders who came with the boots of their cars filled with sacks of kitchen waste, or their roof racks high with discarded consumer durables. Here in the rural depths of the heart of the country, you can put out your trash and wait a week for it to be collected, and in the meantime the dogs, the foxes and the badgers will knock over the bins, rifle the contents, and spread your intimate rubbish over acres. So the communal tips are widely used.

Flora put two boil-in-the-bag curry dinners into the pan of water which steamed on the little peat fire. (Bernard had recently acquired a couple of sacks of burning peat; it burned with a mild heady scent, and left behind dense grey ashes, which she liked.) She squatted before the pan, the skin stretching tight and smooth over her knees. Bernard watched and pondered over his first day's work at Avon Farmers.

'The farmers come up and order by numbers,' he said, 'from the catalogue. I bring out the sacks, that's all. Why do they pay me so much? And why me?'

'You're not straight,' said Flora, 'that's why. It's as Arthur said. You'll keep your mouth shut, if it's in your interest.'

'But about what?' he asked, as if she knew. 'What's in the sacks? This farmer today asked for lactose. Nothing wrong with lactose. It's a form of sugar.'

'Fancy you!' said Flora.

'I did A-level chemistry for a term,' said Bernard. 'I may be stupid but I'm not daft. But this geezer told me the lactose went in the milk, and brought it up to Marketing Board standards. Can that be right? Every tanker he takes in is worth ninety quid. If it's low in sugar content it gets rejected. He wasn't going to throw good milk away, he said. So he just tipped the lactose into the milk and then the results came up fine. If the Milk Board wants sugar, he said, they can have sugar! Why should I be penalized? Why should my cows be insulted? They're good cows and they give good milk. It makes you wonder!'

'Wonder what?'

'What's in the other sacks. Why we stay open at night, and why more people come by night than day, and why everyone pays with cash.'

'I thought all that would be up your street, Bernard,' said Flora, sadly. He was not renowned for his honesty, nor had his father been before him.

'Tell you what,' was all he said, 'don't let's drink milk any more.'

With their curry they drank wine, which Flora had acquired from the Harris household over past months. It had been the Harris habit to buy their wine in boxes. Flora would open the packs when Natalie was out shopping, abstract a third of the wine, refill with water, shake well and then re-seal the containers. No one had ever noticed. It had been Bernard's idea, and seemed to Flora not unreasonable, since she was so underpaid, and recently of course not paid at all.

Bernard put his arm round Flora and they spent a comfortable and cosy evening in the midst of their wasteland, watching the sun sink behind the Tor. Of such pleasures are domestic happiness made.

Attempts at Seduction

Angus went round to dinner at Dunbarton. Natalie had thawed, plucked (badly) and stewed (rather well) the chicken. She'd even remembered to de-gut it, holding her nose. (Her rubber gloves had split: she had no money for new ones. The electricity bill second reminder had arrived, but not yet the red one with threats.) She'd run the tap through the chicken's poor empty sinewy middle. (The water rates had been unpaid for several months: but the Board seemed reluctant to actually cut off supplies.) She'd taken some of her clothes to the Nearly New shop in Wells and Brenda there, knowing Natalie's predicament, had given her a good price there and then, on the spot: she had used that money to shop for vegetables and After Eights.

The children possessed Post Office Savings books, which was just as well. On the day Harry left, Alice had had twenty-three pounds in hers and Ben eighty-five (he would) in his. These sums their mother had persuaded them to part with. She had not returned to the DHSS offices; she was putting that off to the last possible moment, continuing to believe that any minute Harry would ring, or write, or even turn up on the doorstep. If people can go suddenly, they can return suddenly. Inspector Took rang to say Harry had been traced to Marbella but extradition proceedings weren't likely. The inspector, in other words, was prepared to let sleeping dogs rot. Inland Revenue were putting the house and contents up for auction in three weeks' time: Angus was to be the auctioneer. The bank would claim its overdraft, various building societies their debts. These pieces of news Natalie received calmly, as if they related to her dream and not her waking life.

In the meantime Natalie went to bed in the same room, dressed in the same clothes, ate – admittedly cheaper but much the same – food, stroked the cat as usual and weeded the garden. She suffered from occasional bursts of one nasty passion or another.

'How do you cope?' she demanded of Sonia. 'How do you manage?'

'You have no choice,' replied Sonia, bleakly.

Sometimes Natalie would walk to the school with Sonia and her kids, but sometimes she would leave either early or late so as to miss her. She did it on purpose. Alice and Ben were beginning to seem more real and less like marionettes than before, and Natalie now found some comfort in their company. She jumped when the phone rang, half fearing bad news, and half hoping for good. But the telephone bill had gone into the red, and then beyond threats into bold statements of intent and soon would no longer be a source of either fear or hope, but simply of silence.

Well, well! Tonight Angus was coming to supper and leaving Jean behind, on the grounds that Natalie needed help and advice. She was amazed at how simply and easily she managed to prepare and cook the supper. Onions steeped in hot oil, with rosemary from the garden added, the lanky chicken joints rolled in sesame seed and fried with the onions and rosemary, and then simmered for ever in added white wine. The chicken was tough but the flavour was fine; now Harry was gone she could cook. How strange, she thought. Perhaps her fits of rage, grief and resentment were nothing to do with the loss of Harry, but to do with the loss of years wasted in a half life, as half Harry.

But listen, enough about Natalie, Angus is at last talking. Nothing will stop him. He looks at her shyly from time to time. He feels awkward in his body: his tie is askew. He has been up to say goodnight to Natalie's children, to boom at them with an unfamiliar but reassuring male voice. The children's bedrooms are not right next door to Natalie's bedroom: there is a bathroom in between. He is glad of that. He hopes her kids sleep soundly. He realizes his mind is leaping ahead too far and too fast; but then again, nothing ventured, nothing won. And Angus is in a position of power. Even so, he feels tentative and helpful and is surprised at himself.

'Do you have any candles?' he's saying. 'I like dinner by candlelight. Jean doesn't see any sense in it. She's a practical woman. No softness. You're not a practical woman, Natalie, or you wouldn't be in this fix now. The house not even in joint ownership! It was bound to happen. Down comes Inland Revenue, up go the For Sale notices and before you know it your house is sold to the first bidder. Not the best but the first and if word gets round it can go for as little as half market value. Inland Revenue don't care, so long as they get their whack, why should they? There'll be nothing left over for you, if you're not careful. But don't worry, I won't let it happen. I have quite a lot of pull round here. I'm ever so fond of you, Natalie.'

She stares at him with her full blue eyes. He doesn't know what she's thinking. He wishes they could forget supper and go straight to bed.

'What happened between you and Arthur?' He wants to know, and he thinks it would be good to remind her she's not so virtuous as she makes out. Again she doesn't reply. 'Don't bother,' he says. 'I can imagine. Worried husbands aren't much cop in bed. Me, I never

106

worry.' He laughs lightly, to show it's true. 'Harry was a bit of a cold fish, wasn't he. Did he wear his steel-rimmed glasses in bed? Why did you marry him? What got into you? Someone as gorgeous as you? What did you talk about in the evenings? Or did he just watch telly? Anyway, you found a bit of light relief in Arthur. I don't blame you. Except Arthur! – Well, there you go again. A bit of a poseur, really, Arthur. An eye to the main chance, sexually. Not serious. I'm serious, Natalie.'

He finds he is. He doesn't want to go to bed with her now. He's frightened. He wants her to love him, and want him, and when he's sure of that only then he'll go to bed with her.

'Warmth,' he says, out of the blue. 'A man can't live without . . .' He isn't sure what it is a man can't live without, except all the things he'd had to: he lives with a woman set up in antagonism against him; the best he can do with her is a kind of animated, sometimes even exhilarating, armed truce – but what he wants is gentleness, enclosure, love – who doesn't?

'Take me seriously, Natalie,' is all he can say.

And Natalie responded to Angus with what she described later, ashamedly, as a splurge of self-pity.

'You called me Natalie,' she said. 'You called me by my name. There's no one to do that anymore. I don't seem to have friends. There are people who call me Mrs Harris and either blame me for what Harry did, because wives are always held responsible, or blame me because somehow or other I must have driven him away, and the children call me Mum, and now I come to think of it Harry most often called me "you". Miss Eddon Gurney's name is Marion. I expect he's with her now. I expect he says her name all the time. What would the time be in Marbella? They're probably

making love this very minute. Though why should I
think they'd wait for night? If people really fancy each
other, night or day should make no difference, they'd
be at it all the time. Harry and I only ever made love
in bed. Never once out of it. Some people use the bath,
don't they, or sofas, or fields, or floors.'

'When they're young,' he said, cautiously, thinking
of his back. What was she suggesting? But she fell
silent, and wouldn't meet his eye. He moved in to take
the benefit of the moment and put his arm round her
but she stepped away.

'You're taking advantage of me,' she said. Well, what
did she expect? Of course he was, in a way.

'I'm trying to help you,' he said. Of course he said
it.

'You're not helping,' she said. 'How can I explain to
you how my body feels? That if anyone touches it,
anyone gives it a feeling that will upset it, it will simply
collapse and die and me with it. You don't care about
that: you just care about you. You'll help me out, you
say. You'll get a good price for this house. You mean
if I go to bed with you you will. Otherwise not.'

'I didn't mean it like that.' Well, he half had, half
hadn't.

'I don't care what happens to the house,' she said.
'What happens to me and the children?'

'Same thing,' he said. 'Money is what matters.'

'My body matters,' she said, savagely. 'Harry used it
and threw it away, and Arthur entertained himself okay
with it, just for the time being – '

'You were doing the same thing, weren't you?'

'Then I was wrong,' she said severely, reminding
him horribly of his wife. 'I want my body for myself,
thank you, for the time being.' And Natalie shut her
mouth tight; clamp, clamp, in the mood of one fixing

a chastity belt upon herself, iron and unforgiving though it might be. In Natalie's situation, I can tell you, I'd have been in bed with Angus like a shot, and forget his paunch and his maunderings, but not Natalie. Well, some women are like that. Irrational and unrealistic. Fussy, in a word.

'Quite wrong,' Natalie opened her mouth sufficiently to say, before snapping it shut again, and Angus felt defeated, and fat, and unwanted and went home to Jean without his supper. Jean had a period, or so she said. No doubt she had pills to bring one on whenever she felt inclined, which was mostly. He was the more aggrieved because he had felt and offered love.

Arthur lay in bed that night with his wife Jane and thought she was a dear, good creature, and he should behave better to her. She had never, even in her younger days, given him cause for jealousy, and so he scarcely understood the emotion himself, but understood it must be painful and obsessive, or why else was she so thin and jumpy? It was a mistake for her to live above the shop: she should be further away from the back room. Then her mind could be more at peace, and she would not feel obliged to go searching for stray hairpins and long (or worse, short and curly) hairs, which she would then put under a child's microscope in order to identify, by colour. But of course, these days, so many people's hair was multi-coloured.

'Tell you what, Jane,' he said, 'let's rent out the flat and buy something outside Eddon Gurney.'

'Something with level floors,' she said, 'so I can wear heels.'

'Something *new?*' he said, shocked. Then he said, generously, 'But if it's what you want.'

'There's so little on the market,' she said. And there was. House prices rose and rose. Now the trains from

109

Castle Carey and Bath were so much improved, the rich were moving further out of the London suburbs and commuting in to work. It was becoming more and more like Surrey, Arthur complained. But now was obviously the time to buy; just before the property boom was properly underway.

'I'll look out for something,' he said. 'I expect I'll hate it but if it's what you want, that's the main thing.'

He would like her to be happy, so long as her happiness didn't stand between him and his.

Doing it all Wrong

In the middle of March, Ben and Alice started at the comprehensive. That is to say, Ben stood in the playground on the morning of the first day and shouted at his mother, 'I won't go to this school. I won't. I'm not like the others. They're thicks and turnip tops. They'll laugh at me. I hate you! What have you done with my father? You are a bitch!'

Then he gave up, and went inside, unprotected by a school uniform (for here they wore any old thing – one of his other complaints), looking much like anyone else aged 12. Presently Alice stopped crying and went inside the school too, to whatever unpleasant destiny she believed awaited her. Natalie found herself saying under her breath, 'I hate you, Harry Harris' and meaning it.

Hate is the third stage of the cure. After passivity comes anger, after anger comes hate. These allegedly negative emotions are to my mind fine, healing things. Natalie was fortunate enough to heal quickly. People differ in the speed with which they recover from what therapists refer to as major life disasters (divorce, that is to say) in the same way as they do from cuts and bruises, and she was lucky. She had been born with a very strong life-energy (Tor-language – sorry) which during her marriage to Harry had simply stayed tamped down, underground. It was this, I do believe, which made her so attractive to men (oh and women, women too!) at that particular time: the sense of the unreleased, which they (Eros willing) might be the lucky one to

111

release. Her suitors interpreted it as simple sexual attraction, but it was more all-pervasive than that. Oh yes.

Dunbarton was withdrawn from auction, suddenly, at the end of March, and was sold, privately, for sixty thousand pounds.

'He offered cash,' explained the pleasant, bright-eyed young man at Waley and Rightly, the estate agents. He was Angus' assistant. 'We can't afford to let a cash buyer slip through our fingers! Not with Inland Revenue tapping on the window pane! Not to mention the bank!'

Natalie could remain in the house for two more weeks, he said. The contents were to be auctioned separately at the end of that time, and should, he consoled her, fetch an excellent price. Angus was to be the auctioneer.

'A fine man!' said Bright Eyes. 'Splendid auctioneer.'

Natalie went down to the Welfare Office, and this time saw not Mary Alice but a certain Rosemary Tuckard. Rosemary had a flat, round face and very tiny features, so her face seemed almost blank. Talking to her was rather like talking to one of Alice's cut-out paper dolls, Natalie thought. But at least she smiled and nodded, and a cold dark hole did not seem to be her natural home.

'Inland Revenue forced the sale,' said Natalie. 'I didn't have a leg to stand on, according to my solicitor. Not that I trust him. One of his friends bought it, as it happens. You know him? Arthur Wandle the antique dealer? His wife was tired of living above the shop.'

'It's easy to be paranoic at a time like this, Mrs Harris,' said Rosemary Tuckard. 'That's a very serious allegation you're making and I don't think you should repeat it.'

'If I'm paranoic,' said Natalie, 'will I get more housing points?'

She was getting quite sassy with those in authority. It did her no good.

'I wonder if you're being quite open with us about your circumstances?' asked Ms Tuckard. 'A lot of people do withhold information, thinking perhaps it isn't relevant, when it is. If, for example, you are in receipt of any financial help from a man or are even living with one . . .'

– 'I've declared everything and I'm living with no one' –

'Then what *are* you living on?' enquired Ms Authority, 'if, as you say, you have no source of income since your husband left?'

'On the children's money boxes.'

'Um. I believe you did have an association before your husband left?'

Now how could she know a thing like that? Easy. She was a good friend of Jean the pharmacist. Who wasn't?

'Are you implying it's my fault my husband left?' demanded Natalie. She was bright pink and angry. 'Is that what you mean . . . ?'

'Well,' said Ms Tuckard, who had never been unfaithful because the opportunity had never arisen. 'You can't mess up your life wilfully and then expect the State to step in and pick up the pieces!'

'What sort of world is this?' demanded Natalie, flailing away. 'Do I have no privacy at all?'

'It's a world in which you are asking for public funds,' said Ms Tuckard, primly, 'and your character and behaviour when in receipt of them must be taken into account.'

'But what you're talking about was *before* I was in receipt of them.'

'Of course,' the flat-faced woman now apparently in charge of Natalie's life and conduct observed, 'and therefore doesn't affect your legal rights: not at all. Nevertheless, we do have areas of discretion. I take it the sale of the contents is expected to bring in quite a sum?' No doubt she too was a friend of Bright Eyes.

But, as Natalie explained, much of that was already bespoken. The school fees had to be paid, and all the local creditors. It was a matter of pride, as much as legal necessity.

'Pride,' observed Ms Tuckard. 'You may have to learn to forgo that.'

'And after that I'm homeless,' said Natalie. 'That's why I'm here. Not to talk about my love life.'

'You want the children put in care? Is that it?'

'Of course not!'

'It might be best for them until you're sorted out.'

'I don't want to be sorted out, I want a house to live in.'

She was doing it all wrong, of course. I told her so later.

'You mustn't talk about wanting this or that,' I said to her, 'about your feelings or pride or whatever: you must talk about your rights as a citizen half the time and cry the other half. That gratifies them both ways – as officers of the State and virtuous private citizens to boot.' But too late then, of course.

'A *house* is out of the question,' said Ms Tuckard. 'We just don't have houses available. I wish we did. Our public housing stock is being run down. We are obliged

by law to sell them to tenants if they wish to buy, and
round here they often do. The re-sale price can be
really quite good, you see, what with the views and the
scenery and people wanting second homes, weekend
cottages. There is, of course, emergency accommodation. We don't like women and children of otherwise
good character sleeping in ditches! So we do have a
hostel. You have to be out by nine in the mornings,
of course, and not back until seven. It can be tricky,
especially if it's raining, but better than nothing.'

'I suppose I could join the peace convoy,' said
Natalie. 'At least they wouldn't turn me out in the rain.'

'I wouldn't advise it,' said Ms Tuckard, suddenly
brutal. 'They have some very nasty diseases up there.
In fact, if you try anything like *that* we'll take the children into care at once.' And that put Natalie in her
place.

At periodic intervals the peace convoy – for so it
calls itself – trundles into Glastonbury: a procession of
ancient vans and lorries which journey at an average
speed of three miles an hour, wherein the peace hippies
live, in what the good citizenry see as squalor,
depression and aggressive criminality, and the travellers themselves see as pleasant, dozy virtue, and the
only possible way to live – semi-nomadic, looking
always for a home, a place where welcome awaits, and
taps and hot water, and never finding it. Moving on,
moved on, the new gypsies. Well, to journey is better
than to arrive – or so say those who have already
arrived! The peace travellers shake their dreadlocks on
the local streets as they gather before the local DHSS
offices, and wait to collect their rights, their payment
from the State. To the ratepayers, to those with painted
front doors, it seems that AIDS, herpes and hepatitis
fly in a mist about them as they wait. Shop doors slam

and pubs close as they pass. Some have noses eaten away by cocaine and syphilis, some are whole, clean and beautiful and most consult the stars for advice. They have their spokesmen (sorry, spokespersons) and their martyrs. Policemen offer them petrol to take them off to the next county. Vigilantes slash their tyres to show them what is what. Otherwise, nobody knows what to do about them. For what *is* what? How can they be sent back home when they have no homes to go to? How can they take jobs when they don't have the mentality to *do* jobs? How can those who ought to be in the loonybin go *there* even, since they're closing down all over the country, and not just in the heart of it? How can those who should be in prison go to those, since the prisons are already packed to bursting with those who consent to society's reproach, and these do not? You can hold one person against (allegedly) his will, but a hundred thousand? The peace convoy is the first tattered, fluttering swallow of a long hard summer ahead, in which the travelling dispossessed roam the countryside, living off what they can.

Natalie would never join them. She would be too frightened. I toyed with the idea once. But to be outside the law did not suit me. And I'm sorry to say I was swayed by the Argument from Hygiene. I wanted to be *clean*, I wanted not to *smell*, and I wanted that for my children too. That was the real madness. For of course you can't get away from dirt, ever. There's a kind of grime about mental hospitals: a lingering septic smell, like the children's breath when they have tonsillitis. Patients are still put to washing floors, but nobody teaches them how to do it. Washing floors is a skilled job. Most people (like Flora) do it by swilling water around the middle, without sweeping properly first, so that mud lines the skirting of the floor, up and into the spaces between cupboards and furniture. And if you walk down any corridor in a mental hospital you will observe the inch of black grime which proves me right.

Washing Away the Stains

Arthur came to see Natalie on the day the contents of the house were sold around her. She sat in the children's empty playroom. Porters had taken the contents away, and set them up in lots downstairs, under 'Toys – assorted'. Natalie did not mind seeing them go. She hated Ben's Zoids and Action Men and robots and computer games: they were soulless and nasty. They were training her son in murder. She hated Alice's Care Bears and Cindy Dolls and Little Ponies. They were training her daughter in silliness and sentimentality. They could all go. Natalie could have stopped them, and said to the porters, 'No, are you mad? Toys are personal! Not part of the sale.' But what would she have done with them then? She had two big suitcases already filled to the point of not closing. She could take with her, wherever she was going, what she could carry and no more, one suitcase in each hand, like a refugee. Who knew when she would ever again have a shelf for a toaster or a board for an iron, let alone a cupboard for toys! Let it all go, and she would take the money, and start again! She wanted nothing of the past, anyway. The past was all full up with Harry Harris, whom she hated.

Arthur said:

'Natalie, I feel bad about this. But Jane and I were so crowded above the shop, and there was no way you and the kids could stay here, what with the rates and so forth. They are high, aren't they! And whose idea was the underfloor heating? Very uneconomical, and splits the wood if you have good furniture. God knows what I'm going to do about that! But it's taken the problem off your hands, hasn't it, Nat? And at least you know the house has gone to a good and friendly owner for a quick, cash sale.'

'Oh yes,' said Natalie.

'You'll be moving out tonight, I'm told?'

'That's right,' said Natalie. 'Don't worry about me, Arthur. The children are down at the playing fields. I'll pick them up after the sale, and be out of your life, not to mention your house!'

'But not out of my heart, Natalie. You know that. Ever. Where are you going? Friends? Family?'

'Never you mind, Arthur, I'll be all right.' Natalie had her pride, as we know. Not by a flicker would she show that she minded: that Arthur had upset her; Arthur, whose body she had known, had been so familiar with. He with the substantial, friendly girth, with its warm, pleasant smell, and all the pleasure that came with it, and whose mind she had not known at all.

'Anyway, good to know Angus will look after you,' said Arthur, placatingly. 'Since you'll have nothing more to do with me. You'll get quite a bit from the sale, I imagine. Enough to get you settled.'

Arthur had not been attending the auction, Natalie could only suppose, though Jane was down there buying an ironing board for 25p, a box of cutlery for 50p, and a set of chairs for five pounds, or Arthur would have understood very well that Angus was not looking after Natalie. On the contrary. The sale had gone largely unadvertised, and the buyers who turned up were mostly friends and colleagues of Arthur and Angus, or customers of Avon Farmers, on the trail of a bargain, and finding many. The new freezer went for fifteen pounds, Angus seeming unable to hear a call of twenty pounds, coming from a man who just happened to be passing, had seen the crowd, and stopped, and now couldn't believe his luck. It must be something about the acoustics, he supposed, which made the auctioneer keep missing his bid.

'Do you like gardening?' Natalie asked Arthur, as she picked up her suitcases and prepared to leave.

'No. But Jane does.'

'Good,' said Natalie, leaving Dunbarton for the last time. 'This place could be made really nice. You never know what you've got till it's gone!'

She was right. I sit here writing in my cubicle, with the peephole in the door left over from the old manual days, so the nurse could look in to make sure the patient wasn't swinging from a hook in the wall. She can do that now by looking at a screen, for we are all electronically surveyed, but the peephole remains, in affectionate memory of the past. There's a central locking system so the duty nurse can lock my door from a distance any time there's trouble anywhere, or she thinks there might be. Clunk-click! I too think of what I failed to appreciate. I have always wondered how it is that one guard can handle so many prisoners; why there are not more army mutinies, more prison breakouts, why the massacred stand idly by and let themselves be massacred? It's not just guns and gas and superior muscle power that does it. A critical mixture of coercion and persuasion is no doubt required: and superior knowledge and technology on the part of the warders comes in handy, but it is the fixed notion of guilt on the part of the prisoners that really does it. They have done wrong: therefore they deserve to be badly treated. They are badly treated: therefore they have done wrong. And the unfortunate construe their misfortune as their own fault, and so consent to their incarceration. I sit here on the bed, writing, submitting to electronic surveillance, because somehow I think it's what I deserve, and because look, it's better than loneliness. Anything is. Those who are watched are not alone!

Natalie was walking down to the playing fields with her suitcases when Angus drove up in his Quattro. He had created an unscheduled interval in order to pursue her and speak to her. She should have been flattered.

'I'm sorry,' he said. 'I'm really sorry. I've been childish and vindictive. Jean always says so. She must be right. I shouldn't throw my weight around like this. I can't stand rejection, that's what it is, and you were really rough on me the other night. Still, what we got today should see you right. Deposit on a home. Unless you're off to join Harry? I assume you are. That's what it's all about, isn't it?'

'No,' Natalie said. 'It's not.' (Natalie always spoke the truth – I sometimes think for lack of the wit to do otherwise – and so was always believed.) 'And what's more you won't even reach four thousand today, Angus, and I owe nine thousand in debts. There's still a minus balance.'

'Christ,' he said. 'Natalie, I'm sorry.' He was, too.

Unlike me, Angus had no trouble feeling remorse. But too late, of course. The thing about remorse is that it's a perfectly safe emotion. It always *is* too late.

'Where are you going?' he asked. 'To friends?'

Natalie thought a little.

'The thing about friends,' observed Natalie, 'is that I suppose I could say Jean and you were our friends, and Arthur and Jane. So on the whole I'd rather stay with enemies.'

'You're something else,' he said, in admiration, as

she walked past and on, and into the playing fields
where the Quattro couldn't follow, or not without
damage to its paintwork. He went back to the auction,
and let the prices run in Natalie's favour. He would
earn her love, somehow, now he had worn out his
malice.

Shock

Natalie came to live with me. Not before she had moved into the council hostel, of course. She collected the children from the playing fields and with a suitcase in either hand walked on into the Emergency Hostel in Eddon Gurney.

'Why didn't you come straight to me?' I asked her later.

'I didn't like to,' she said. 'Anyway, they were expecting me.' A feeble answer, but then she was tired. She'd been allocated a room in Redfield House, once a convent, now roughly converted to multiple use; one family to a room, and communal cookers in the corridors, out by 9.00 in the morning and not in before 7 in the summer, 6.30 in the winter.

'The worst thing about the hostel,' Natalie said, 'was that they'd painted bright colours over dirty walls: yellows and pinks and greens, in the hope of cheering the place up. But it was beyond cheering, and so were we.'

Well, that was her point, wasn't it? She wanted to be really worthless, really degraded, really at the bottom of the pile, our proud Natalie. Really finished. That's how the end of a marriage takes some people. They find themselves cleaning other women's houses, or with some horrible skin disease, or whoring to make ends meet – anything to punish themselves for their failure. Failure? Well, of course. Their failure to be loved, every woman's task, duty, to find someone to love them.

Dragging the kids along as often as not, to witness the punishment.

Natalie had just stood there, since Harry left, and let herself be cheated, robbed, insulted and misled by Arthur, Angus, Alec, the bank manager, the police, the school, the DHSS – everyone. You could hardly blame them for doing it. She was like one of those little dolls weighted at the bottom, the only point to whose existence is that you try to knock them over. The dolls come on up again, swaying and smiling – they're vaguely female – but Natalie was doing her damnedest to stay down.

It was Ben and Alice who shocked her back to her senses: so she shot suddenly upright and this time stayed there. Their poor white traumatized faces stared at her from the bunk beds – inmates had to provide their own sheets and she'd brought these in the suitcases. The hostel kindly provided charity blankets. (Now everyone with any sense uses duvets there's a glut of discarded blankets all over the country and they're freely available.) Natalie was just sitting, too tired even to unfold the rather stained sofa bed and get onto it and go to sleep. She couldn't turn the overhead light off: a greenish ten watt bulb glimmered permanently overhead. The light stays on in case the children wake in a strange place and are frightened, or that's what they say, but they don't mean to make these places too comfortable, do they, or who'd make the effort to get out of them? 'Their faces were so greeny-white and ghostly, and they were so quiet, I realized what I'd done,' Natalie said. 'I realized they only had me. Harry wasn't coming back to rescue us. I clapped my hands and said very loudly, 'All right! Up! We're getting out of here,' and they both sat up at once.

'Natalie,' Ben said, 'I think we'd better stay just for

the night. Get some sleep. We'll think in the morning.'
(it was the first and only time he ever called her Natalie.
Usually it was Mum, or Ma, or You. (The softer form,
Mummy, was left for Alice.) But now he spoke to his
mother as if she were an equal. This shocked her, too.
Between them, Harry and she had deprived their son
of his childhood – not that he'd been making too good
a job of that, either, to date. Privilege and self-doubt
mixed makes some people obnoxious. and Ben was one
of them. In the short time he was with us up at the
estate, he improved enormously: privilege had been
snatched away, and his sense of being the one male
amongst so many helpless, hopeless females did
wonders for his self-esteem. He was okay, was Ben, in
the end.

'No,' said Natalie, 'we're going right now! We are
simply not going to spend the night in a place like this.'

And the children dressed and Natalie packed, and
they tiptoed down the yellow and pink stairs (no
carpet) in the greeny light from the horrible unquenchable bulbs. The warden – I shall call her Ms Frostbite
because I never did get to hear her name – popped out
of the ground floor front room where she was watching
the late-night horror (no doubt) and said:

'Where are you going? What irresponsibility is this?
How dare you take those children out after bedtime!
Don't you know that room was booked for you? Don't
you know by accepting it you were keeping others out?'
and so forth, but Natalie took no notice and kept on
walking, and so did the children, and the door closed
behind them and no one followed them, and they were
free. In the dark, in the cold, penniless, hungry, and
alone, but free.

It took them forty-five minutes to walk to the Boxover
Estate. Once they heard a police car, and hid behind a

hedge until it passed. Perhaps it was looking for them, perhaps it wasn't. Were there laws concerning vagrancy? Natalie didn't know. There was a full moon. There was almost no traffic. The countryside seemed to hover – as if the fields lay quivering an inch or so above the brown earth – patterned with strange silvery shadows. Natalie had never seen it like this before. Even the children were impressed. 'It's like fairyland,' said Alice.

'You're such a baby,' said Ben, but he said it kindly. He carried one of the suitcases. Alice helped Natalie with the other, and though this was more trouble than it was worth, as the corner of the case kept banging into her ankles, Natalie did not try to stop her. Neither child complained about tiredness, hunger or thirst, and now they were out of the hostel and their mother was in charge of them and herself again, the colour had come back to their cheeks, albeit a strange translucent moonlit pink, the like of which Natalie doubted she'd ever see again. Crunch, crunch, crunch went their footsteps, echoing. An owl hooted, a fox barked.

'I like this walk,' said Alice. It was their moment out of time.

Her knock got me out of bed. Knocks after midnight usually mean trouble. I opened the door and there Natalie stood in the moonlight with her children, half apologetic, half stubborn. She didn't say anything. Her presence explained itself.

'Oh well,' I said. I was wrapped in my blue silk kimono, circa 1930, 80p from Oxfam. 'End of a quiet life. Come in. You can have the sofa, the kids will have to make do with the floor.'

You've got to stick together, down here at the bottom of the world. As I say, all you have in the end are your friends.

Interlude

Of course Sonia loved Natalie. Of course she was in love with her. Wouldn't you be? Who else was there for her to be in love with? Some women can't go out their front door without meeting up with a randy wood-carver or an alcoholic one-eyed sailor, while others get into a state where they only ever meet other women. Men somehow dissolve out of their life altogether. This had happened to Sonia. So when Natalie knocked upon her door in the middle of the night, wide-eyed and dramatic, what did you expect would happen?

Don't misunderstand her. Sonia would no more have *touched* Natalie than have picked up a dog's turd with her bare fingers, even a dog she knew well. She would, that is to say, have considered any kind of physical approach shuddery, and she certainly could not imagine *kissing* Natalie. Sonia would have found the deed embarrassing and disgusting. Sonia was no lesbian. On the other hand – now, how can she explain this to you? – Sonia could quite see herself in the same bed with Natalie, clasped, clasping and intertwined, giving and receiving all kinds of pleasure, in imitation of the act (as she remembered it) with men: in the interests of comfort, consolation, present-quenching excitement and emotional and physical gratification. But not somehow *kissing*.

Sonia is a disturbed woman. She does not act the way the consensus agrees that a woman should feel and act. That is to say if she kills someone she should feel remorse. If her children are taken away from her she should feel grief. If she takes money from the State she should feel gratitude. If she falls in love with another woman, admit she is a lesbian. Sonia just won't.

What strikes Sonia is how un-free any of us are, to act, be and feel the way we want. Things are offered, then snatched away. Sex with a man gives you such a stunning sense of safety. There you are, suddenly the size of two people, not one: not frightened any more, totally loved, needed, used, valued. As long as it lasts. It's an illusion, isn't it? It stops: it presents you with perfection and then snatches it away. He rolls off and away and you're half what you suddenly perceive is your proper size, and he's back to his wife or his bank balance or his mates or whatever it is that's preoccupying him. How quickly, as young girls, you lose your rightful expectations. Your first lover isn't likely to be loving, tender, permanent, true, is he? The statistics are against it. It's your uncle or his best friend or your best friend's boyfriend, or you're gangbanged or taken for a laugh or so drunk you can't even remember except you're pregnant. And it's a loss. It's a real loss. Why is it men pay so much for the privilege of deflowering a virgin? It's because they're getting real value for money. Virginity is real, it's a proper state, all rightful expectation, and self-righteousness, not just the run up to being fucked by all and sundry. This is why Sonia is glad Stephen has custody, care and control of Teresa, Bess and Edwina. Sonia has no illusions left. Little girls need illusions. Stephen will do them very well: he is all expectation and self-righteousness – look how he behaved over Alec. His daughters will learn from Stephen and look after their virginities until they're ready to hand them over to nice, caring, loving, boring permanent men. If they stayed with Sonia they'd be running after strangers in no time at all, in order to talk to them, and take their sweets, and go behind the bushes, never to emerge again.

Okay, give Sonia a fix. What loathsome drug is choice for today? Go ahead, poison her, calm her, finish her off. It's all attention, isn't it. Attention-seeking devices, like all you Eddon shrinks with your Eddon Method. Goodnight. Sonia will try and do better tomorrow.

Second Home

So there Natalie was the next morning, sleeping on
Sonia's sofa, with Ben and Alice in sleeping bags on
the floor amongst the uncleared-away toys, and a little
white kitten, rashly strayed in from next-door's garden,
batting one of Alice's curls against her ear for the
pleasure of watching it bounce back. At least it was one
step up from the Emergency Hostel – though it was
not clear from Ben's waking expression that he thought
this was the case. He had a clear view underneath
the sideboard to a collection of dusty socks, little girls'
knickers and random female rubbish. At Dunbarton
furniture was properly pulled out and swept behind.

In the kitchen Sonia was trying to muster seven bowls
for cornflakes.

'It can't be permanent,' she said. 'But I expect I can
sort you out. You've come to the right person. I'm a
one-woman Claimants' Union.'

'I'm grateful,' said Natalie.

'Don't ever be grateful,' said Sonia. 'You have to
learn not to be grateful or it'll be the end of you. You'll
sink into the Supplementary Slime and never crawl out.
Cultivate resentment. It gets you further.'

'I'm afraid I'm putting you out terribly,' said Natalie,
in her genteel little girl's voice.

'You are,' said Sonia, 'to be blunt. The DHSS aren't
going to be too happy to discover I'm harbouring a
fugitive from the Hostel. The way they'll look at it is,
what right do you have to turn your nose up at the
taxpayers' offer of accommodation? And they'll find

ways of punishing me. They might even stop my 20p a week soap powder allowance. I get that for Edwina's sheets. She wets the bed sometimes. Does Alice wet the bed?'

'Of course not.'

'Pity. You're really missing out. Does Ben have asthma?'

'No,' said Natalie.

'Encourage a wheeze or two,' said Sonia, 'if you can. They really go for asthma up the DHSS. Instant sympathy. Sometimes people die from it, you see, and they don't want to be blamed, or thought hardhearted.'

'I don't want to be dependent on the State,' said Natalie.

'Who does?' inquired Sonia, civilly. 'But what choice do you have? There's no fresh milk, only powdered. It's cheaper. Ben can make it up.'

The children didn't go to school that day, and Natalie just slept and slept, in Sonia's bed.

Driven Mad

Natalie stayed with me for three months. I gave her tutorials on the Welfare State: she did the things I was too depressed to do, such as picking up toys, sorting out clothes, and weeding the garden. Within the week, strangely, the house had the same polished orderly look that characterized Dunbarton. Very boring. Alice slept with my three, Ben had a blanketed-off section of the bathroom, and Natalie and I shared a bedroom. (Oh yes, separate beds. Are you *mad?* Ros across the road had a divan to spare. She'd found it in a skip. The things people throw out!)

Natalie got thirty-seven pounds forty-three pence from the State, plus various renewal and heating allowances. I managed to extract fifty-five pounds forty-three for my lot. We pooled the money and even occasionally managed a bottle of wine. I don't think she was happy, but I was. No word came from Harry Harris. The children no longer asked after him. Ben was silent but responsible (as responsible as any male can be: that is to say as long as it suits him but not a moment longer: consider his father!) and Alice clucked around my three making herself useful. I could see panic in her blue eyes, sometimes, when she thought no one was looking. Both children hated their school. They were laughed at on two counts: first for having posh accents, then for living on the Boxover Estate, where the new poor (us) and the problem families (her: she'd walked out of the hostel) were housed. Most children adopt the local accent pretty quickly, as cover, but these two

seemed unable to do so. They were somehow
unbending: stubborn, like their mother. They found it
difficult to admit defeat.

Natalie got herself put on the housing list, though I
couldn't see the reason for it. It seemed to me we were
doing pretty well as we were. Only once did she flip.
We and a group of others were queueing outside the
telephone on the green, with our coins at the ready,
and Ros came out of the booth in tears. Ros had a
boyfriend at the time they reckoned was supporting
her, though he wasn't; he could only just support
himself and his beard. So they'd stopped her benefit.
The DHSS don't mind if men visitors stay until two
o'clock or even three, but four's going a bit far, five
smacks of early shift, and anything later means breakfast, and if it's breakfast there's hell to pay. They don't
begrudge us a spot of sex – it saves paying the
psychiatrists' bills later – it's relationships they can't
stand. They reckon the ultimate obscenity is human
affection. If a man stays, your benefit stops. We, the
abandoned mothers of Britain, don't deserve love. We
had our chance, and we muffed it. I muffed my chance
of being kept by Stephen by having this fancy about
Alec, this stupid feeling that even as a non-earning
citizen (stay-at-home-wife) and mother (forgive me,
unpaid child minder for the State) I was entitled to love
and be loved.

So I would get confused and upset sometimes, and
even with my help Natalie got a lot of things wrong.
She should have gone to Welfare in the first place –
they'd have presented her case to the DHSS and the
Housing Department themselves and then both would
have coughed up. And she should never have believed
Mary Alice about Housing: clerks in one department
have no idea what goes on in another, and sometimes

not even their own. Regulations change every week. If you don't hear what you want to hear you must go from clerk to clerk and department to department until you do. Of course Welfare's in Street, DHSS in Glastonbury, and Housing in Shepton, and Appeals in Bridgwater – that's a forty mile round trip from Eddon Gurney, and none of us has a car, have we? And there's only one bus a day, if you're lucky, so you have to hitch, and you can't hitch with children. And that, if you ask me, is why one in five women on supplementary benefit ends up in mental homes. Driven mad by the State.

'Driven mad'. It's just a phrase these days but I think it's a real enough concept. Women do get driven mad. Men drive women mad. Anxiety about how to keep a home going for the children drives women mad. Unrequited love drives women mad. Working out how to get from A to B when you have no money and there are no buses drives women mad. (Don't ask me what drives men mad. Let them look after themselves. They run society, don't they, not to mention the hospitals and the drug industry? They *are* the psychiatrists. How many women shrinks in here? Four? To twenty-eight men?) Okay, okay, feminism sends women mad. Funny joke. Point taken. I have to take it, don't I, because I want to get out of here.

As I say, it was Natalie's turn to flip when we were waiting in the queue for the telephone one Monday morning. I'd been explaining to her how I meant to get through to Tania Rostavitz, the only welfare officer at Gurney who has a clue. That is, by saying I was her sister Anna. I just happen to know, from reading the holiday postcards in her office, that Tania has a sister Anna. Claim a personal relationship – otherwise the switchboard just leaves you hanging on the end of the line, until your money runs out and the pips go and you give up. Saves them all kinds of trouble, doesn't it!

Anyway, Ros came out of the box in tears – you should see Ros: she's so romantic looking: really beautiful with misty black hair and big eyes; she looks like a Hardy heroine, and here she was, stuck with the kids in a council house, arguing with the State as to whether or not this fat, awful little creep with the beard was a full-time or a part-time lover – oh yes, we get reduced by our circumstances! A lovely brimming saucepan of hope and emotion simmered down and down until it's a sort of greasy sludge – if you'll forgive a metaphor from the kitchen. And Natalie suddenly for no apparent reason shrieked and started banging on the telephone box and shouting 'I can't live like this. I won't!' and ran back and sat in the garden all afternoon. Just sat. She wouldn't go inside the house. She said it frightened her.

The only upshot was, of course, she and I had to join the telephone queue again the next day and by then Tania had gone on holiday (they're always on holiday or on courses or being transferred to head office) and there were even more delays. But she had to get through somehow. For some reason of their own the DHSS had given a special clothing allowance to Ben but not to Alice. Something to do with him sleeping on the bathroom floor and her having a proper bed. But by then anyway Alice was sleeping on the sofa. And when we wrote them letters all we ever got was one of those forms with reasons for disallowance on them, and the section ticked 'child over requisite age' which was crazy, since Ben was older than Alice anyway. Once their computer starts doing that kind of thing, you have to get through in person. It's full time work being on social security. They really make you earn your living.

But look, it was cosy. I reckon we could have gone on like that forever. But fate started intervening, working itself up towards the fire on the float. Just little straws in the wind. Natalie actually getting a job and then the odd matter of the old leather bucket. It quite frightens me how *things* keep turning up, and taking a hand in events. You get the feeling that not just people, but material objects, are part of the general conspiracy to toss you up in the air and land you where you least expect.

Cough, Cough, Cough Again

'Same old floor, same old mop, different owner,' said Flora to Jane. (Remember her? Arthur's long-suffering wife? Too thin for her own good?) Now Jane and Arthur were living in Dunbarton, Flora still came up to clean. Why not? A job's a job and it's stupid to feel loyalty to one employer just because they're hard done to by the next. When did an employer ever feel loyalty to an employee? That's what Bernard wants to know. His father worked for thirty-five years in the sales office of a firm which made linoleum. The office was just under the factory chimney. Strange particles fell from the sky, and drifted through the windows, along with the flecks and grime. In the thirty-sixth year Bernard's father got cancer of the lungs. He was fired (before he had time to make a connection between inhaling fumes and his illness) on the grounds that he'd been pilfering. It was true. He had. He'd been pilfering for twenty-four years. Everybody did it. Just a square yard or two of reject stuff, otherwise thrown away. It just all of a sudden became a firing offence, the day after he reported sick. Funny, that. Cough, cough, cough he went and did the new staff-relations man come and visit him in hospital? Like hell he did. A friend or two from work came. A new man sat at his desk now, they said. The waters had just closed over Bernard's father's head. It was as if he had never been. And no pension either, because of the pilfering. And as everyone knows, lung cancer can happen to anyone, even non-smokers.

'I must have been mad,' said Bernard's dad, 'cough,

cough, cough!' He'd never smoked in his life, or drunk, or run after women. 'Thirty-five years of my life, believing if I did my best by them they'd look after me. You take a lesson from me, lad. Don't you believe them when they say a steady chap sticks to one job, doesn't chop and change. That's employers' talk.'

'Chance would be a fine thing,' said Bernard.

'Cough, cough, cough,' went his father.

And now here Bernard was, while Flora cleaned Jane's floor, heaving sacks of enigmatic powders off lorries and on to shelves, wheeling half-corroded drums of liquid from shed to shed, and the only safety measure he could see was a tanker of water and a hose.

'Just dilute,' Angus had said. 'That's all you ever have to do – dilute.' And the previous day one of the drivers had remarked:

'If you get any of the dust on you, wash it off.'

'What sort of dust is it?' Bernard asked. 'Has it a name?'

'Search me, old lad,' the driver said, in the tones of the upper classes. Quite the little yuppie he appeared, but then nowadays men out of universities do drive lorries. They have to. It isn't that the class system is breaking down; no: it's just that those on top, feeling uncomfortable, lean down the ladder and grab what traditionally belongs to those on the lower rungs. Such as jobs.

'All they saw fit to tell me,' said the new-style lorry driver, 'was if you get any of it on you, wash it off lickety-split. I am passing the information on to you, as is only my duty. We working men must look after each other, now they've cut the Factory Inspectorate by 50 per cent and those that are left are kept occupied plugging the leaks in Sellafield pipes. How do you tell a Factory Inspector? His thumbs glow in the dark. Heigh-ho!'

'Twat,' muttered Bernard, ungratefully, as the other drove off.

Now Flora, for her inexpert but frequent washings of the Dunbarton kitchen floor, was these days using a string mop and an old leather bucket. Leather, thought Jane, in this day and age!

'I thought I'd thrown that old bucket out,' said Jane.

'I brought it back in,' said Flora. 'I like it.'

'Then you're the only one who does. It was in a job lot of bits and pieces at the auction. Whoever bought it actually went to the trouble of leaving it behind. That's really saying something!'

'It looks like an antique to me,' said Flora. 'Perhaps your husband would be interested.'

'No,' said Jane, sharply. She did not care for conversations with the help. She did not particularly like the house now she was here. Arthur's furniture looked peculiar in a modern bungalow, even she could see that. Heels marked the parquet floors. She had believed that living above the shop had fuelled her paranoia: she could see that living at a distance from it was even worse. She was fifty. She had done nothing with her life, except agitate about Arthur and sweep a few floors. They'd had one daughter, Carla, now at college, whose existence seemed merely to spur Arthur on to take an interest in younger women. Carla had been her father's child from the moment she first opened her hooded infant eyes, treating her mother with a kind of idle contempt. Terrible, thought Jane, not to like your own daughter, but there it was. She didn't think Carla noticed.

'If he isn't interested,' said Flora, 'my boyfriend will be. He's an antique dealer, too.'

The bracketing of Bernard, king of the rubbish tip, with Arthur, king of Dunbarton, was not music to Jane's ears. No.

Natalie's little grey cat sat looking up at Jane Wandle with wide eyes, reminding her of every young woman who had ever stared thus at Arthur. How the creature got in was a mystery. Jane had sealed up the cat flap, closed the ever-open window of the laundry, but there the cat somehow managed to be, staring up with a look of dependence and hostility mixed. Jane opened the back door and smacked the creature out.

Flora protested. 'You shouldn't do that! This is her home. She's got to have somewhere to live.'

'Natalie Harris should have thought of that,' said Jane. 'If she cared for it she should have taken it with her. Cats are expensive. Why should I take it on?'

Jane thought these days that Arthur probably had indeed had an affair with Natalie Harris. She was his type; little girl impassive, clear-skinned, like one of the dolls she, Jane, collected. For all she knew Arthur was still seeing her.

'Just because you don't like Natalie Harris,' said Flora, 'is no reason to take it out on the cat.'

'Why should I not like Natalie Harris?' asked Jane, a rhetorical question to which Flora replied with a smirk which unfortunately Jane saw.

She was right, then. And moreover, if Flora knew, everyone knew. What could she do? Nothing. Where could she go? Nowhere. All she could do was follow the advice given to economically dependent female spouses since the beginning of time – wait for her husband to cease his wanderings, and be as loving and loveable as possible in the meantime. Jane handed Flora a scrubbing brush.

'I pay you one pound twenty-five pence an hour,

Flora,' she said. 'Please earn it. Use this, if you don't mind, not the mop.' Flora dropped the scrubbing brush in the bucket so that dirty water splashed Jane's nice pale blue floral skirt. 'Some things just aren't worth the money,' Flora said. 'Personally I prefer cats to people! Wash your own floors.' And she walked out. But she took the bucket.

'Of course I'm not having an affair with Natalie Harris,' said Arthur, in bed that night. 'She's not my type. I like skinny women. How you do worry yourself! I think she's having a fling with Angus, actually.'

'What about Jean?'

'Jean won't worry. She's too sensible.' The bed they lay in had belonged to the Harrises. It was king-size, and had gone for a song at the auction. The original Wandle matrimonial bed had fetched five hundred and forty-five pounds a couple of weeks before they'd moved into Dunbarton. How a convenient fate played into Arthur's hands!

A buyer had come into the shop, looking for just such a rare brass bed, and Arthur had taken him upstairs and shown it to him: a splendid piece of brasswork, early nineteenth-century.

'Just as a matter of interest,' said Arthur. 'Of course it isn't stock! Very much not for sale!'

But he'd capitulated on being offered five hundred for it, five hundred and forty-five if the buyer could take it there and then in the van. He could, said Arthur, and when Jane came home from hearing reading, the mattress and bedding were on the floor and her and Arthur's marriage bed of 26 years' standing was gone. She'd cried, and Arthur had been abashed and apologetic, and had had a word with Angus, and was only too happy to buy her the Harris bed when the opportunity arose, which he thought she'd really like, it being modern. (Jane kept saying she hated old things, which in an antique dealer's wife can only really be interpreted as hostility. Can this marriage be saved?)

Now he wondered on which side Natalie had lain, and which side Harry, and why it was married couples stuck to one side or the other, and what was to be made of it.

'I wish you were happier,' he said to Jane. 'I wish I knew what to do to cheer you up.'

'I don't like the house,' she said. 'I know I wanted it but now I'm here I want to be back in the flat. It's too far from anywhere. I can't get proper help in the house and I'm lonely.'

'If that's what you really want,' he said, rather too quickly, 'we'll put the place up for sale right away. I reckon we can get a hundred and twenty thousand. That's sixty thousand clear profit. It's a family house – we can wriggle round capital gains tax on medical grounds, I should think. Your nerves, perhaps – '

'But what will people think? Poor Natalie Harris – '

He was quite taken aback, surprised at the speed of her mind.

'Poor Natalie Harris? Don't spare a pang for Natalie Harris! When the heat dies down Harry Harris will turn up in the north somewhere, with a new name, and she and the kids will be off to join him. It's a set-up job, don't you see? The factory closes, the staff aren't paid, he's got a chunk put away no one can touch. Oh, she's in on it, all right. What did you think she was, a poor wronged woman alone in the world?'

He could not add that since Natalie cheated on her husband she deserved no pity, but he said it in his heart. He wished he had a wife he could confide in fully. He wondered what it would be like to be lying now next to Natalie, and wished he was. Then he fell asleep.

No 'For Sale' board went up. It would have caused talk and speculation. Arthur just had a word with Angus at Waley and Rightly, and Angus said he'd do what he could. Arthur offered a 25 per cent commission, which seemed reasonable inasmuch as it was Angus who had arranged for the house to be sold to Arthur, at, roughly, half its market value. Though a new selling price of one hundred and twenty thousand was pushing it, said Angus. The second bathroom was like a box. But then when did Arthur never not push a profit to its limit?

Traumas

Natalie went up to the Abbey grounds to see Peter the groundsman. He swept; she walked along beside him. She had collected her DHSS draft and had managed to give Sonia the slip somewhere in Glastonbury. Ben and Alice now walked home from school by themselves; Ben put up with the embarrassment of being seen with his sister with the merest shrug, as if this was the least of his troubles. Sometimes Natalie could hear him through the bathroom wall crying in his sleep, but by day he was brisk, competent and distant, and seemed to make no distinction between Sonia and his mother, which might have been an elaborate act of revenge or might not, how could Natalie tell? Certainly he blamed Natalie for so carelessly losing his father. As for Alice, it was hard to tell what went on in her head. She sucked her thumb, and played with Teresa as if she were the same age and not four years older, and pulled Edwina's hair when she thought no one was looking. The clear-eyed, protected look had gone. Alice no longer prattled, but whined. Perhaps she was just growing older; perhaps she was deeply traumatized? Who would ever know, who could ever tell?

'You ought to tell them about Harry,' said Sonia.

'But I have nothing to say,' said Natalie.

And indeed, what was there to say? 'Your father really loves you.' Absurd. 'He really loves me.' Nonsense. 'He's coming back soon.' Unlikely. 'He's gone mad, had a brainstorm.' Lies. He'd left her and the children in the shit and buggered off and what was the point of talking about it. Least said, soonest mended.

She'd written to Harry's father in Geneva, finding the address by chance on the back of a Christmas card envelope while she was packing up Dunbarton, and there had even been a reply. No, he hadn't heard from Harry, nor did he expect to. He was sorry to hear what had happened but the state of his health and his finances would not allow him to get involved. Piss off, Natalie, in other words. She hated Harry and hated to see him in her children. She grieved for them and was cold to them at the same time. Just as Sonia saw Stephen looking out of the eyes of Teresa, Bess and Edwina, Natalie saw Harry in Alice and Ben. Once you have children by a man, that's it. You are never free of him, unless you can free yourself of your children too. Chances are you can't. Chances are they'll turn up at your funeral and throw a rose or so into your grave.

Sonia gets on all right without her children. If they want to strike up a relationship with her when they're teenagers and can wipe their own noses that's fine by Sonia. Their stepmother, Sandy, is okəy. Sonia used to know her well. Steady, Catholic, moral, plain, doesn't say much but tidies up a treat. Will suit Stephen down to the ground. Sandy will never be found *in delicto flagrante*, or *in flagranto delicte*, or whatever, when Stephen goes to open the back of the family car. Sandy will never crack sour jokes and upset people. Sandy will stop Edwina painting her toenails and backcombing her hair at the age of five. Five, yes. Was four, is five. Sandy will have given Edwina a birthday party. Stepmothers are always in the business of doing better than the mother. Sandy will have put up with the racket and boredom and mess of the party without a murmur. *And* cleared it up, quick, so Stephen could stand in front of his hearth and have a quiet glass of sherry before dinner. Let Sandy do it. Good luck to her. She'll need it. It's Sonia the kids will want later. Sonia will never lose them now. Those you want for ever, give away. Like boomerangs, they'll return.

Sonia hopes Sandy made the cake herself, that's all. That it wasn't a shop one; not for Edwina, who's so special.

Here come Sonia's pills. She needs them! Goodnight.

Bright and Purposeful

Where did I leave Natalie? Why, up in the Abbey grounds, chatting to Peter in that rather cosy, companionable way which means you want a job and the other might have one. 'There's a waiting list for working here,' said Peter. 'And the Abbey Fathers are very traditional. Outdoor work is man's work, so far as they're concerned. But you could try up at the quarry, if you're desperate. Emphysema land.'

'Emphysema?' Really, Natalie knew nothing.

'Dust in the lungs,' said Peter. 'Kills you in the end. But by that time you've got your cards, and are off. Why should they care? And what can they do about it? Spread used tea leaves when they blast, to keep the dust down?'

'I've just got to get myself out of this situation,' said Natalie. 'Since there's no one to help me I'll have to help myself.'

'Try the quarry then,' said Peter. 'The Devil helps those who help themselves.'

Since taking his advice, although it was always enigmatic, had turned out well in the past, Natalie took it now and the next day went up to that part of the old quarry which was still being worked, in the section of the hill above Bernard and Flora's caravan. White dust shrouded the road and fields for yards around. It crunched underfoot as Natalie walked. Sirens sounded, and a whole section of Somerset hillside crumbled and collapsed in its own special granite cloud. A line of ancient giant rock-crunchers prepared to receive that

day's splendid dinner. The ground shook beneath her
as the rock fell away.

'Okay,' said the site manager to Natalie. 'You want
to be the gofer? You be the gofer! You're here in person,
which is more than can be said for the one we employ
now. No phone call, nothing! Can't say I'm sorry; his
mum's up here all the time, about one thing or another.
The trouble with today's young, they can't tell a job
from a classroom.'

'What will I have to do?' She had no idea, but she
was astonished and gratified to find a job was so easy
to find.

'Make the tea, run errands, copy out the work chits.
Can't use a computer out here: the dust gets into the
works.'

'And the lungs,' she said, coughing, but he didn't
seem to think that was funny. Not one bit.

'Shift work Monday to Thursday: 6 a.m. till 2.
Thursday through Saturday: 3 to 11. Forty quid.'

'The day?'

'The week,' he said. 'No arguments. Take it or leave
it. If you don't take it someone else will.'

'I can't manage on that!'

'Lady,' said Bob, for so he was called, 'that's no
concern of mine. Try for Family Income Supplement, if
it's not enough. Don't expect me to keep you in luxury.
Start on Monday.'

'All right,' she said.

'Where do you live?' he asked, in rather more friendly
tones than before.

'Eddon Gurney.'

'Oh, Eddon. No bus. I'd give you a lift up in the
mornings but the wife wouldn't like it.'

'I'll manage,' said Natalie.

Now what Natalie failed to notice, being not, as we

have observed, the most perceptive or sensitive girl in the world – in spite of what I've said to the contrary in the past, in Natalie's defence: I do think it takes a pretty obtuse kind of person not to notice when a husband plans to leave – was the flash of the Quattro round corners and hedges wherever she went. Angus was well and truly hooked on Natalie, as men can sometimes be on women whose moral approval they want. Of course Angus wanted her body – who wouldn't? – but he wanted her to like him, approve of him, admire him and tell him he was doing just fine, as well. All those very reactions, in fact, a man can reasonably expect from a wife, but seldom gets, and Angus certainly did not receive from Jean.

'I reckon you're a closet queer,' Jean would say, blaming him for her lack of orgasm.

'You were a fool to buy this car,' she'd say, every time the garage filled it up yet again. 'More money than sense!' 'She'd never look at you, you're past it – an old man with a paunch,' she'd say, if he admired some woman on TV. 'Why can't you take up an honest profession,' she'd say, if he pulled off some stupendous property deal.

'Big fish in a little pond,' she'd say, if he got his name in the local paper. And if he gave her a cheque, out of the blue, she'd say 'Now what are you trying to buy?' Or if he bought flowers, 'What have you been up to, Angus?'

What he liked was Natalie's silence, her soft, occasional glance towards him, the tremble of her bottom lip, how feeling hard done by, as she must about the auction, she had not ranted or raved. She wouldn't talk to him, true, but she'd get over that. Moreover he had let it be known to Arthur that he and Natalie were in what Arthur liked to describe as a 'leg-

over situation'. He wanted it to be true, he was humiliated that it wasn't true: he meant to make it true.

So when Natalie left the quarry in the pouring rain
and started walking down the hill, it just so happened
the Audi Quattro happened to be passing.

'Give you a lift, Natalie?'

She'd said no often enough on the road to school,
outside the house, by the post office, and at the shops,
quite automatically. Now her lips seemed stiffened by
white dust and she needed shelter. She stayed quiet
and just got in. 'What are you doing here, Natalie?'

'I've got a job.'

'What do you want with one of those? Do you no
good. Wear you out.'

'I want to be independent.'

'Why didn't you tell me? I thought all you girls together were happy enough living off the State. I could
get you a job.'

'What doing?'

Angus thought fast.

'We're entering a float for the Carnival. Needs
someone to be in charge – what's wrong with you?'

'No, thank you,' said Natalie.

'No strings attached,' he pleaded.

'No.' She didn't even bother to think about it. She
just said no. It annoyed him.

'Eighty pounds a week, cash, no tax deductions.'

She shook her head. He wanted to shake her. He
took her back home, or to her half-home, down at
Sonia's. The Quattro had parked outside better places,
his expression said. Slumming, where the little children
swarmed, and all of them fatherless! As are 23 per cent
of all the nation's children of course, but someone like
Angus wasn't counting. Takes a mad woman in a
loonybin to actually count. One child in thirty these

days is born physically handicapped. Did you know that? Sonia saw it on a poster only yesterday. And no money for research any more. The only people doing research are the drug companies themselves – the ones who make Thalidomide and allied substances. That's the way it goes, these days. For the heart of the country read the pocket of the country.

'Any time you want out!' Angus said. 'But I suppose you two ladies are snug enough,' and he was pleased to see Natalie reacted to that. Just a spot of colour in her porcelain cheek, but nonetheless a reaction. She had lost the dishevelled look of the early days of Harry's leaving, he was sorry to see. Except for a little patch of quarry dust left unbrushed on the side of her skirt, she was otherwise well turned out. When it rained the dust would turn not so much to mud as to a thick gluey paste. No brushing it off then. It won't be long, thought Angus.

Sonia too knows what it is to love Natalie, to want to raise a spot of red on the porcelain cheek.

Bargains

In the meantime, Bernard has gone up to Arthur's, there in the shadow of Gurney Castle where the cobbled streets meet the ancient castle walls, and all is grey, grey, grey, except for Arthur's yellow waistcoat when he comes outside to arrange his wares. Bernard dresses in leather, and other mirk, as befits today's dustbin young. It's their elders who bounce about on lively polished toes in bright, soft wools and won't be defeated. Bernard had brought with him the leather bucket recently appropriated by Flora; his purpose was to flog it to Arthur.

In order to enter the shop Bernard had to pass through Arthur's outside wares – today including a rather pleasant but battered games table: a japan box with broken drawers and an over-varnished pig bench with a cracked basin and ewer upon it. Arthur would put such bargains out of doors, hoping to get rid of them quickly, before their sorry state finally defeated him, and he sent them off to the restorers, spending more on them than he was ever likely to get back.

A certain Sandra Radlett came out of the shop as Bernard went in. She was twenty-two or so, with a clear skin and wide-apart blank blue eyes: like a doll, Bernard thought. He wondered what she was on that had made her pupils enlarge. (The young notice things like this.) He supposed sex could do it. Arthur pecked Sandra Radlett on the cheek, patted her on the bottom and said:

'Now don't get serious. We're in this for laughs.' She

tittered obligingly, nervous of Bernard, and left. Sandra worked in the bank, and took a late lunch on Tuesdays and Thursdays. Jane no longer lived above the shop, of course, but Arthur was a man of habit.

Arthur did not seem pleased to see Bernard. He knew trouble when he saw it.

'Why aren't you up at Avon Farmers?'

'I'm on nights.'

'That's promotion! Time and a half! Congratulations.'

'It's okay if you've got no principles,' said Bernard, and Arthur thought he was joking, but Bernard was serious, and taller than Arthur, what's more. 'Trouble is, I have.'

'Cheap food for the millions,' said Arthur. 'That's what this country wants, that's what this country gets. Down there at Avon Farmers you're doing your bit for Britain.' And he laughed.

But Bernard just went on staring, so Arthur stooped and took the leather bucket. 'Funny old bucket,' he said.

'Georgian, I reckon,' said Bernard.

'George the Sixth, yes.'

'Leather. Not many of these about.'

'They're all over the place,' said Arthur. 'Common as mud.'

'Twenty quid to you,' said Bernard.

'You're joking. Couldn't raise a tenner on it. It's been about. I've seen it somewhere.'

'Couldn't have,' said Bernard. 'Turned up on the dump. If you're not interested, I'll take it somewhere else.'

'You're going too fast,' said Arthur. 'That's for when I say twelve and you come down to eighteen, and neither of us will say fifteen. You're losing your cool. But you have an instinct. Tell you what, we'll make it fifteen, and when you're finished at Avon Farmers I'll take you on as my assistant.'

'Finished? Is there something you know I don't know?'

'All good things come to an end,' said Arthur. 'Even Avon Farmers.'

'What are you talking about?' asked Bernard. 'Nerve poison?'

Arthur sighed pointedly and handed over three five-pound notes for the bucket and Bernard said:

'And another eighteen. That's what Mrs Harris owes Flora and never paid.'

'Why should I pay Natalie Harris' debts?' Arthur was afraid of the answer but couldn't help asking.

'Because you bought her house for sixty thousand and a couple of months on you're selling at one hundred and twenty, and that's sixty thousand clear profit and I reckon you can afford it.'

Arthur paid up.

'I worry about you, boy,' he said. 'Good thing there's no Mafia round here or you'd end up head first in a drainage dyke.'

Ah, the heart of the country!

Gratitude-Schmatitude

Natalie's job. She shouldn't have taken it and I told her so. She had no social conscience at all – or else she was just naive. Up at the quarry they were lowering the going rate every month. Now it was down to just two pounds a week more than the basic benefit and women like Natalie still turned up to take it, beaming their gratitude.

'It's better than being on the dole,' said Natalie to Sonia.

'No it isn't,' I said. 'Did he mention Family Income Supplement?'

'Yes.'

I explained and explained that FIS was a hidden supplement for employers, but she couldn't seem to grasp it. Somewhere inside herself she was still on the employers' side. A good night's sleep or so and some help with the children and a suitor to reject, and she bounced right back and looked and acted as if she belonged to the haves and not the have-nots. FIS, I explained, was for nuclear families, the inept but good, not the abandoned mothers, the sloppy and bad. I asked her who was going to look after the kids – me? And she said she'd manage, and I said she meant I would. I asked her how she was going to get to work each morning. I asked her where she was going to live because it certainly wasn't going to be with me, because people were saying she and I were lesbians and although I for one didn't have anything against lesbians, I didn't want Stephen to turn up and take away the children because of my immoral life.

I got a spot of pink on her cheeks all right. I got her waving her arms around, bright pink and shouting stop it, stop it, stop it. I put my arms round her because I was sorry I'd done it and she pushed me away, saying:

'Don't *do* that,' and I hated her. This love business doesn't flow the same way round all the time. The energy flows the other way and you hate.

There's a lot of energy floating around here. It pours out of the Tor, on just a few days every year – you can feel it. Even though the sun's rising in the east and the Tor's in the west it still manages to cast some kind of shadow over you. On those days I'd keep the kids off school and we'd all go off to Weston or somewhere for the day. You can hardly swim, it's not the South of France, but you can watch the rip tides, and look up the numbers drowned that year. That day I didn't have the fare to Weston – they'd put the fares up again. I just had to stay home and face myself and try and meet the energy from the Tor. The house is bang on a leyline. Not good. It's better to be just off it. Open the front door and the back, on some days, and you can practically see, feel, touch the Powers walking through it, pacing on their march from here to there, balancing the Universe. Nonsense, but true. Or as they say of the cream cakes – naughty but nice. On other days, open both doors and all you get is a draught and a flurry of waste paper.

While Natalie was screaming her head off in my house and thinking perhaps Angus was a better bargain than sharing with a lesbian lunatic, Bernard had gone back up to Flora with a bottle of champagne. I'm glad her life then wasn't all bad. I say that, but actually think champagne's acidy stuff and not a patch on a good claret. My father (allegedly) drank himself to death on good claret. Bernard was talking, as men will, about the moral dilemma he found himself in and Flora, as women will, was suggesting he just got on with the job in hand and stopped yacketing and boring her to death.

'They wouldn't be allowed to sell it if it wasn't safe,' she said.

'They aren't allowed to sell it. They just do. Preferably by night, because then the customers think they're getting a bargain.'

'It's just business,' said Flora. 'Private enterprise.'

'I suppose it's regular employment,' he said. It was an attempt to cheer himself up, but it didn't.

'Just be careful,' she said, 'not to get any of it on you.'

She put down her glass and wandered over to her little patch of cultivated garden, where a bumblebee hummed amongst some rather exotic triple tulips. She'd brought the bulbs home from Dunbarton in the brief interregnum between Natalie and Jane. The limey soil at the base of the quarry seemed to suit them, or was it just having their freedom, for now they were out of their plastic pots and into the wild windy spaces, and they were doing very nicely indeed.

Bernard began to laugh.

'Now what?' she asked. It was getting dark. The bumblebee buzzed off home.

'I sold old man Arthur his own blinking bucket back,' said Bernard.

'You shouldn't have,' she said, and she shivered. 'You're too clever by half. It's unlucky, that kind of thing. Something always comes back and hits you in the face.'

'You're soft,' he said. 'Daft.'

Arthur took the bucket home to Jane. He thought

she'd like it. He'd sold her Victorian-over-Georgian silver teapot the week before and she'd wept. It was a hideous ornate thing but obviously exactly what one particular buyer from Maryland, over on a visit, would pay well over the odds for. Such an opportunity was not likely to come Arthur's way again for some time.

'But it looked so nice on the mantelpiece,' she moaned.

'It looked terrible,' he said. 'And you know it's stock; only borrowed for the house.'

'Everything's stock,' she said. 'Everything I like at any rate. You do it on purpose. I expect you think in your heart I'm stock too, and you'd sell me given half a chance.'

He would, too, he thought, but he knew better than to say so. What's more, you could find a buyer for almost anything in this world, if you just waited. There is almost nothing nobody wants. People would buy half an old shoelace, if they thought it was a bargain, and use it to tie a rose tree to a stake. A lot of people would think Jane a bargain, and he knew it. Loyal and true and concerned.

'Jane,' said Arthur, producing the bucket, 'I thought you might like this. Georgian. Lovely piece of leather work.'

Jane laughed and laughed. Arthur wriggled.

'You've been had!' she said. 'Someone's finally sold you back your own property and you've been too greedy to notice. How much did you pay for it?'

'Practically nothing,' said Arthur, but he was lying, as we know. As it happened, he *had* paid well over the odds, being partly afraid, partly admiring of Bernard. The swagger of mirky leather jackets, the gleam of buckles and zips, strike awe and envy into the soft bright elderly. That's why it's done.

Arthur didn't stay in that evening. He said he had to stocktake, and young Sandra Radlett came round to the shop after the bank closed and Jane wept alone amongst her parquet floors. Wives shouldn't gloat and be nasty, especially when their husband's professional pride is at stake.

Angus, passing Arthur's shop that night, saw a light on and knocked. Arthur peered out from the back and, seeing Angus, came out and let him in. Sandra Radlett had just left. She had to be home before her husband. Angus caught a glimpse of narrow skirt and neat legs as she departed. Sandra favoured navy blue, white, pearls and low-heeled shoes. But she had lots of long hair she wore up, the better for her husband (and Arthur, and others) to let down.

'Stocktaking?' asked Angus, full of envy.

'What else!' said Arthur, and both men laughed.

'I've come about the low image of estate agents, developers and so forth,' said Angus. 'WAEADA's got to do something.'

'Oh-um,' said Arthur. 'What do you really mean?'

'I mean,' said Angus, 'the Young Farmers are backing out of the carnival. They're sulking about milk quotas.'

'Quotas kill,' said Arthur, 'and all that.'

'All that,' said Angus. 'So there's a half-built float going cheap. WAEADA can take it over.'

'Who's got time to do it?' asked Arthur. 'Not me!'

'You might find time,' said Angus. 'Cut down on the extra-curricular activities.'

Arthur owed Angus quite a big favour, what with the sale of Dunbarton, the king-size bed with its memories of Natalie, and so on.

'I couldn't do that, Angus!' protested Arthur. 'What do I know about carnival floats?'

'Put the women onto it,' said Angus. 'Keep them out

of trouble. Give Jane an occupation. Poor Jane!' He smirked. Arthur writhed. What could he say?

'Bill Radlett's a member of WAEADA,' added Angus. 'Just joined.'

'I'd no idea,' said Arthur. 'But his wife's not. That's the main thing! A carnival float! It'll cost money,' he added, hopefully.

'Waley and Rightly have a Carnival Fund,' said Angus. 'As from today. You won't be out of pocket. You could put Natalie Harris in charge.'

'Ah,' said Arthur.

'Get young Bernard to tow the float up to Avon Farmers,' said Angus. 'They can use the spare barn up there.'

'Is that wise?' Arthur worried about what was in the sacks. Bernard wasn't the only one. Everyone has a conscience. Only the sum at which it cuts out differs.

'Safe as houses,' said Angus. 'We're switching to the orthodox stuff, anyway. Legit growth promoters, cut-price fertilizers, all that. Then we'll phase out altogether. Someone wants the site for a Garden Centre, come the autumn.'

'Thank God for that,' said Arthur, whose land it was, leased to Angus, bought cheap on a lucky impulse some years back.

'It's Greenpeace here and Friends of the Earth there and who's to say they're not right?'

'Agitators and alarmists,' said Angus. 'What do they know about agriculture? Now Hinkley Point! There's something to really worry about. If something happens at Hinkley Point what happens to property prices round here?'

Hinkley Point is the local nuclear power station. Various incidents in the past have rendered a number of its concrete pipes twisted and crooked, but British

Nuclear Fuels assures everyone this in itself is no kind
of hazard and who is to say they are not right? Environ-
mental groups disagree, but then this is in their natures.
Local newspapers run the story bottom left on the
second page if it happens to come up. But that was
where Angus always looked for really significant
stories. He wasn't daft.

Submission

Natalie had finished work for the day. Her second week's pay packet was in her pocket. The total was twenty-three pounds fifty-six pence, after National Insurance money and tax at the emergency rate had been deducted. She was walking home, since the one bus which passed the quarry gate came at eight minutes before the 6 o'clock siren went, and it was Natalie who was expected to push the button for the siren. It was raining. Natalie wore an old raincoat (two pounds seventy-five pence) and rain hat (seventy-five pence) and a pair of walking boots (one pound twenty-five pence) bought from Oxfam with Sonia's help. The hat was inadequate and the rain made pasty runnels down her face, where quarry dust still lingered. There was no shower on site, and if there had been it would not have been available to females, in the interests of common decency. The job was terrible. Natalie's task was to run here and there in the rain with cups of tea and messages, diving for shelter when the dynamite sirens went. Someone else was always there to push those – that was fun. When the sun came out others did the messenging and Natalie was put in the sweltering Portakabin to work the switchboard. Gnarled men clumped about disliking her, and younger, redder ones muttered about women taking the bread out of the mouths of family men. Nobody even whistled at her.

Angus' Quattro drew up beside her. She consented, once again, to get in. She had a blister on her left heel from the boots and from the feel of it the plaster had slipped. Otherwise she would just have shaken her head and walked on. But if she kept walking now she would be in worse pain tomorrow, and if she did not work, she was not paid. On such small choices are our futures determined, and not just ours, other people's.

'You can't go on like this,' said Angus. 'Your face is thinner. You'll get old before your time.'

'I don't have much choice,' said Natalie, but no one likes to hear that time is overtaking them. If you drudge for a living you end up like a drudge. She remembered her mother telling her this, and for the first time for years, years, missed her mother. Tears of frank self-pity came into her eyes.

Angus – he drove casually, one-handed, and at unnerving speed – put his spare hand on her knee.

'There, there!' he said, and Natalie felt a rush of not quite affection or dependency, but a kind of sensuous, erotic helplessness.

'What you need is a man to look after you,' he said. 'Heard from Harry?'

'Of course I haven't heard from Harry. Have you?'

'Why should I hear from Harry?' He sounded surprised.

'Because I reckon you and Harry made a deal. Harry disappears. Tax man claims: knock the house out to Arthur. Re-sell: split the difference three ways. Re-appearance of Harry, tax paid and twenty thousand to the good. And he does you a good turn next time.'

'There's a flaw in that somewhere,' said Angus, laughing. 'But you're learning.'

'What's the flaw?'

'We wouldn't go to all that trouble for so small a sum.'

She didn't appear convinced.

'I suppose I should be grateful he didn't insure my

life and then murder me. Just drop me at the gate, Angus. I'm not asking you in.'

'I don't want to come in.' He took two twenty pound notes from his wallet. 'These are for the kids.'

She stared at the notes and then put them in her pocket.

'How's your wife?' she asked.

'Much as usual,' he said. 'Shall I take you out to dinner tonight?'

'All right,' she said, giving in. I think it was the sight of the notes that did it. Up at the quarry she got paid in fivers and pound coins. The sight of large denominations can act as an aphrodisiac. 'Pick me up at eight.'

She came into my house with the light of treachery, that is to say heterosexuality, in her eyes.

Normally she came in exhausted, white and depleted, and would sit down in a chair, arms and legs dangling like one of Bess' rag dolls, and let me make her a cup of tea, which she'd drink while the children stared. But on this particular evening she came in quite cheerful and animated, and when she bent her head over the sink to shake the quarry dust out of her hair, it was as if she shook off depression, need, the past, everything. Perhaps it was just having forty unexpected extra pounds in her pocket, but I think it was more the reviving effect that the prospect of an erotic adventure has on women. I should have noticed and known.

Jealous and resentful? Of course I was. Who ever wanted to pounce on me in the hour of my greatest need and offer me a way out? Who ever followed me down country lanes in an Audi Quattro, or lay in wait in the alley behind the International Stores? I deserved good fortune, and got none. Natalie, who turned out to be nothing much better than a whore, deserved nothing and got everything. She left her children for me to look after, while she worked (of course I looked after them: what else could I do!). She had no community spirit: she took a job which fellow feeling with the hard-done-by should have prevented her from taking. She used my house as if it was her own. She used my heart as if it were hers to use and abuse as she felt fit. When it came to it, I just didn't count. If a man turned up, any obligation to a female friend simply fell by the way. It was inexcusable.

I told her so that evening. She went into the bathroom looking like a Moscow street cleaner and came out dolled up, in a tight black skirt (hers, from the Harrix days) and a frilly white blouse (mine, Oxfam, one pound eighty), and make-up (Marks & Spencer, bought at the school fair for four pence – the blue eyeshadow all gone but everything else okay). She'd washed her hair and towelled it dry so it was curling wildly. She looked terrific. We were meant to be having split peas and sausage for supper. I'd planned it. I'd been soaking the peas all day.

So when she came out of the bathroom I was startled and asked where she was going.

'Out to dinner,' she said, without so much as a by-your-leave.

'You didn't ask me if I'd babysit,' I pointed out.

'I'm sorry,' she said, not sounding sorry at all. 'I didn't think. My two are old enough to leave anyway.'

'That's hardly the point,' I said. 'I've made a special meal for us and now you're letting me down.'

I shouldn't have said it. I shouldn't have been so neurotic. I should just have let her go, happily. I couldn't.

'I'm sorry,' she said. She wasn't sorry at all. She was embarrassed.

'I don't want you to be sorry for me,' I said. 'I just

want you to have a scrap of feeling for me. But you don't. You use me, you make use of me, you'll go out to dinner but you won't think of taking me. I'm not good enough for you!'

And so on and so on, weeping and wailing. Absurd. The kind of thing wives shriek at husbands, or, I suppose, any spouse or partner of any sex who's on the losing side. It's a kind of madness. Every word you utter, claiming love, makes you the more unloveable. The children looked on, trying to puzzle it out. They hadn't seen me like this, weeping and hysterical, ravenous for love and reassurance, since their father left. They'd almost forgotten. 'Don't leave me, how can you, you don't love me, my life is wasted – ' Did I drive Natalie further into Angus' arms? Probably.

When she was gone Ben said, 'Shall I make you a cup of tea?'

During his stay with me he had become a much nicer child.

Seduction

You know how these things go! First the dinner. Angus took Natalie to the Skinflint's Arms, Wedmore Way, where he thought there wouldn't be too many friends and acquaintances about, and the ambience was cosy and the food good: that is to say, cooked rather than microwaved. Jean microwaved everything. She was too busy, she said, to do anything else. She would drive to Yeovil on Thursday afternoons (her half-day off), park the car on the double yellow lines outside Marks & Spencer, and stock up with frozen food. If Angus wanted anything different, said Jean, he should buy and cook it himself, particularly the former. She gave the parking tickets to Angus to pay. Angus ate out a lot, which seemed to suit Jean, but not normally in the company of young females. Though he doubted if she would have minded that either. He would have if he could, but he did not possess Arthur's easy charm. Now, facing Natalie, Angus found his hands trembling as he handed her the menu. He was not as used to this kind of thing as he would have liked.

Natalie ran her eye briskly down the columns, stopping where the numbers were biggest. She had the crab cocktail, the fillet (not the rump) steak, and a *crème brûlée*. She asked for champagne cocktails to begin with, and Chateau Neuf du Pape '79 with the meal. She ate ravenously and drank heartily.

'I've been living on lentils,' she said. He didn't know what lentils were. How could he?

'If I'm drunk,' she said, 'I can't help what I do, can I?'

That encouraged him.

He said he had a nice little flat in Wells, going free; a luxury holiday let, overlooking the Market Square. Four bedrooms – 'Oh, goodie, one for guests', she trilled – fitted kitchen, bath with shower, heated towel rail – 'Heated towel rail! Oh, fab!' (was she laughing at him?) – view of cathedral and fully furnished to the highest standards. A new firm-but-soft Relyon bed in the master bedroom. Jean insisted Angus and she lie on an orthopaedic mattress for the sake of their backs. The only thing that ever gave him backache, he could swear, was lying upon it. 'Double?' Natalie presently inquired.

'Of course it's double,' said Angus. 'There are always double beds in master bedrooms.' She *was* laughing at him.

Why? Her eyes were too bright. She kept touching him, speculatively, with her little fingers – more reddened and chapped than he remembered, but then quarry work's tough, especially when the weather's bad, and it had been the worst summer in living memory. Bess, Teresa, Edwina, Alice and Ben had all been cooped up together when by rights they should have been out in the garden. If the weather had been better, I reckon Angus' luxury flat wouldn't have been so enticing. View of Cathedral is all very well; but the noise! the traffic! Anyway, I blame the weather. I'm tired of blaming people.

'You can have it free until November,' said Angus, hedging his bets. 'I'm not losing out. The tenants paid in advance then never turned up. After that, it's winter rates.'

'And by November you might be tired of me,' observed Natalie. 'Heigh-ho!'

'I'll never be tired of you,' said Angus, and took her hand next time she touched him. She did not pull it away.

'The only thing is,' he said. 'Will you want to leave your lady friend? Tucked up there so snug and cosy, the pair of you!'

Did she deny me? Did she say I was a fat, garrulous, semi-mad succubus, and she couldn't wait to get out? Did she say she was driven mad by my lesbian advances? By the shrieks and the rows? No, I don't think so. I think when he asked that – and ask he had to – she said something like, 'I'll be sorry to leave Sonia. She's been very good to me. It's just we're so overcrowded, and what with money being short and the weather so bad – '

At least I hope so. You have to believe well of at least some of the people some of the time, if you're going to have the courage to live amongst them. Bill Mempton says sanity is returning. What on earth makes him think that?

It was Natalie's idea that they go and seal their bargain – that is, her body for his flat – up on the tussocky grass at the foot of the Mendip Mast.

'Why there? It'll be cold.' He'd had in his mind a rather nice little furnished cottage near Crosscombe, of which he had the key. The tenants had been gone only a couple of days, so it should still be warm and cosy.

'There's a moon,' she said. 'And anyway it just feels right.'

She didn't suggest Glastonbury Tor, did she? Though the grass there is just as tussocky and smooth. She knew well enough she'd be struck dead for unrighteousness, for confusing sex with a business arrangement. Her instinct was right. The broadcast messages radiating out from the Mendip Mast – Songs for Swinging Lovers and the EastEnders and the stock market prices – have somehow got into the landscape round the Mast, which was well-suited to the occasion: an uneasy mixture of sentiment, worldliness and greed.

Angus was right, too. It was cold and uncomfortable at the foot of the Mast; the sense of electronic humming and buzzing all around and Natalie's goose pimples and little cries, caused not by him but by gravel and stones against bare skin, made the occasion less than satisfactory. Nevertheless it was a start; it felt like an affair beginning – not beginning, climaxing and ending all at once. Natalie bruised easily. She talked while she made love: she practically chattered. He liked that. Jean never made a sound.

'You do talk a lot,' he said, when he was driving her back to Sonia's. Natalie was extracting a piece of gravel out of her leg. She had not bothered to put her tights back on.

'I think what it is; you really like me. You pretend you're doing this because you have to, but really you want to.'

She just laughed, and gave a little yelp as she finally squeezed the gravel from her leg.

'Am I better than Arthur?' He wanted to be.

'Everyone's different,' she said, declining to gratify him. But he was: or perhaps they both were, together. Natalie had her own theories on sexual attraction. She told me about them when I went to visit her later in her love nest in Wells; she spoke with the kind of irritating authority women have when they're in the middle of some swinging affair, and are speaking to friends less blissfully (or so they see it) situated. With Harry, she told me, sex had been frequent at first, and

then dutiful: a matter of proximity and cleansing rituals.
A lot of toothbrushing, and armpit washing before and
after. In its way it had been exciting, because the need
for hygiene had made the act seem dirtier: and the
emotional distance between them the greater, inasmuch
as how could the Harry of his orderly, conventional
days be related to the Harry of his silent, sinful nights?

Arthur? Arthur made her feel wicked, not dirty.
She'd stand in the back room of the shop in broad
daylight dressed only in a slip. He'd take it off her,
staying fully dressed himself. He hardly bothered to
take his trousers off. She did what he said. There was
a kind of languorousness about it she loved. I know
the feeling. It's what I had with Alec, only more so.
Meet me here, he said. You do. Meet me there. You
do. Who cares who's watching? Do this, say that, feel
this, think that, open your legs. You do. It's insensate,
hopeless love – it's a disease. It's caught from other
people, just like measles. It passes, like the measles,
but sometimes, in the meanwhile, damage is done.
(Measles may be a childish disease but it can blind you,
deafen you, kill you, too, in the passing.) You're as
much in control of yourself while it lasts as if you're
running a temperature of 105. You lie down, toss and
turn, burn and freeze, moan and groan – pity is needed,
not reproach. Pity and a cure. Natalie was infected by
Arthur. Harry leaving had been her cure. Instan-
taneous. It shocked her back to sanity. Next time she
saw Arthur she couldn't remember what it had all been
about – perhaps because actually the sexual satisfaction
had been minimal; she needed the act like an addict
mainlining to stop the distress, rather than get a high.

And Angus? Well, that worked, Natalie said, because
he made some kind of connection between her and her
body that Harry hadn't, and Arthur hadn't. She wasn't

afraid of him, as she had been of the other two: she half despised him and half liked him. She hoped for nothing, she thought the situation was ridiculous, she enjoyed herself because she could see she might as well. She looked forward to her new flat and knew it was hers as long as she wanted it: and it gave Angus so much pleasure to plunge around inside her she couldn't help liking it too. It didn't sound to me like true love but it sounded okay.

When she got back to my house, all flushed good humour, I had a shock waiting for her. Oh yes. I was waiting up to deliver it.

'Natalie,' I said. 'You had a visitor when you were out. Did you have a good time?'

'I'm sorry, Sonia,' she said (smug bitch!). 'But yes I did have a really good time. Who was the visitor?'

'Your husband.'

That got to her. Colour drained from her face – all that endearing pinkness – and she looked like the quarry drudge once again, the Natalie I knew and loved.

'What did he want?'

'He wants the children to go and live with him in Spain.'

Well, that's what he'd said. He hadn't said anything about wanting her back: on the contrary. He didn't look guilty or distressed. He'd looked prosperous and healthy, if furtive. Knocking on my door after dark, frightening me out of my wits! Ben and Alice were both sleeping on mattresses upstairs. He'd gone up to look at them. I asked him not to wake them, and he didn't. But he'd seemed shocked to see them on the floor.

'She's not fit to look after them!' he said, and then, 'Is it just you and your husband?'

'Just me,' I said.

'Just you and her!' he said, with meaning. And then, 'Tell her I want the kids. Tell her I'll be in touch. Out on the town, I suppose! I must have been mad to think I'd find her in.'

He wanted it both ways, I could tell. He wanted his abandoned wife to be not only a lesbian but also a heterosexual nympho. In other words he didn't like her very much. He'd walked out, and she was taking the blame for it. He didn't seem a particularly pleasant person to me. I told him he was polluting my house and asked him to go, which he did. Miss Eddon Gurney 1978 was waiting for him in the car outside. I caught a glimpse of her as I slammed the door. 'Poor old Nat', I'd thought, along with 'serve her right'.

'He can't have them,' Natalie said. 'He can't have the children. I won't let him.'

Hi, Dad!

Sonia helped Natalie and the children move into the love nest. Sonia was a good sort before she became a murderer. Sonia gritted her teeth and put up with her own disappointment, and the prospect of loneliness once again. You can be lonelier with three small children than without them. It's something to do with the burden of perpetually looking after, never being looked after. Sometimes, it's true, Bess would make Sonia a cup of tea, and Sonia would have to try not to cry, from the sheer relief of it. (Okay, self-pity. Long sad notes on the violin, and so there should be. Poor bloody Sonia, say I. She had a raw rough deal. She got mixed up with bad bad men: the kind who destroy with smiles and self-righteousness, so you don't know you're under attack until it's too late.)

Sonia consoled Natalie by telling her that in a time of low female employment and low female wages (same thing) an ordinary woman had these alternatives: she could live off the State or live off men. She could not take the middle way and live off her wages. Natalie had tried that, hadn't she, and failed. So now she was the auctioneer's paramour.

Sonia suggested most forcibly to Natalie that she let the children go with their father. What sort of life could Natalie offer them? What sort of future did they have in this worn-out, sold-up, clapped-out country? Not even a change of government could save it now. Too late! Drug addiction, cancer, suicide all epidemic

174

amongst the young! At least their father had a swimming pool.

Oh, but Natalie was stubborn.

'My children have got me,' she said. 'I'll work for them. I'll see them through.'

'You can't,' said Sonia brutally. 'There's nothing here for the young. Look what they've made of us! A nation of whores and criminals. I cheated on the bus on the way up here. I got away with someone's thrown-away ticket. I'm a criminal, you're a whore.'

'I prefer the word paramour,' said Natalie, primly.

Angus came up to the flat two or three times a week. Jean knew all about it.

'Can't you even park your flash car discreetly?' was all she asked. 'Does it have to be right outside her door? Everyone knows. It's "Oh Jean, saw your husband's car in Wells' market again: Oh Jean, I thought you ought to know." ' Jean slept soundly enough on her side of the hard orthopaedic mattress, in spite of her protests. Angus thought if she lost no sleep over it he could be doing her little harm. Sex with Natalie made him want sex with Jean, but if he approached her she'd shrug him off saying he was too old and fat to be the great lover, and please not to paw her about, for God's sake. She was tired and had work to do. Angus thought perhaps he might ask her for a divorce, but he feared her tongue if he broached the matter. He didn't like the way Alice and Ben looked at him, either. Alice stared reproachfully with her wide blue eyes, so like her mother's, and Ben with a steely hostility as if he, Angus, was a debtor, and Ben the creditor. And they would quite deliberately make holes in the carpet with the toes of their shoes. Luxury flats were not really suitable for children: the carpets might look thick and rich but in fact were flimsy, and the same went for the rest of the furniture. Only the bed was solid, soft and fine: just about double enough. Sometimes they ended up on the floor; but with her stifling her laughter, her moans, for the children's sake. One way and another, Angus agreed with me that the children ought to go, before Harry changed his mind.

'But he's a criminal,' Natalie would protest. 'And they're all I've got.'

'You've got me!'

'We *want* to go,' the children said. That was a shock. Ingratitude! Alice would come home crying from school, Ben would return sulky and bruised. Alice stole sweets from Woolworths (Alice, stealing!), and Ben's homework was never marked because of the teachers' strike.

'I'll never get any GCSE's at this rate,' he said. 'I'll work in a factory all my life. Well, that's what you want! That's your ambition for me!'

'I don't,' she'd protest.

'You do,' he'd say, bitterly. 'You hate me because I'm my father's son.'

Oh yes, oh yes, Ben and Alice wanted to go all right. Here was Daddy, offering a villa on the Spanish coast, complete with swimming pool, money, sun and status – he sent them letters and photographs, and also once an appalling little note on scented paper from the beauty queen, saying she knew she could never take their mother's place but she wanted to be their friend. And what could Natalie offer her children? The prospect of living in a holiday flat in Wells that lasted as long as their mother's relationship with a married man, and consequent nudges and giggles at a school they hated. Of course they wanted to go. Wouldn't you? Look at it their way. Their mother had driven their father, by her unfaithfulness, into the arms of another;

had discouraged him so that his business failed; had given away the family dog; had let the family car be repossessed – and what else? Oh yes, had disgraced them by working up at the quarry, by living off the State; had made them sleep on mattresses on the floor and taken them out of a school where they were happy and put them in one where they were miserable, to be laughed at by thicks and turnip tops. No, Ben and Alice were not pleased by their mother. Some children (not all) find themselves extremely offended by parental misfortune.

The only problem to my mind was, in the end, why did Harry Harris want them? Ungrateful little brats.

In the end Harry won and the children went. Natalie let them go. They cried when they hugged her goodbye. They left from Bristol Airport. Angus drove them there in the Audi Quattro, and they kept putting down the electric windows on the way so the upholstery got spattered with rain. They knew that life was a fight, and they meant to win it: they would swim forever in their father's swimming pool – he who knew how to enjoy himself and how to get out of debt quick. Angus spent all that Saturday night in bed with Natalie and most of Sunday too, and did not have to pretend to be just another visitor. He no longer blamed Jean for not having given him children. Natalie wept and mourned and raged a little, but in an agreeably sensuous manner. She needed comfort and he gave it to her.

Interims

And that's how it happened that between March and mid-October Natalie lost a husband, a home and her children, and gained a flat in Wells and a lover from Eddon Gurney. That's how it happened that, by the end of October, Natalie was earning one hundred and twenty pounds a week working on the WAEADA carnival float in the big barn adjoining the Avon Farmers' depot. She'd struck up quite a friendship with Flora's Bernard. She would paint and hammer and upholster and he'd filch paint remover from his shelves so she could clean her hands, and tools to make her life easier. The advantage of an organization like Avon Farmers is that they don't account too carefully. They rake in the money without too much fuss. Bernard would bring her his worries, along with their wares. She was an older woman, but not so old he didn't enjoy her company.

'Do you think I should walk out of this job?' Bernard asked Natalie one day. Her mouth was full of upholstery tacks. She was making a swan-shaped stool in white velour, on which Mrs Housewife Princess was to sit. 'And not just wait till it happens?'

'Why in particular?'

'New Wonder Bio-Eater. Sounds like a soap powder but it isn't. Mix with water, one part to twenty, allow five minutes to work. Twenty millilitres makes 250 gallons. Must be quite strong, don't you think?'

'They wouldn't allow it if it wasn't safe,' said Natalie piously. Everything I told her about the world had just passed in and out of her head. She was doing nicely, thank you. She'd got her freedom and her youth back; she was earning well: she was having a riotous sex life and not caring one whit about her lover's wife. She was never one to think very far beyond her own interests. 'Bio-eaters eat antibiotics. Farmers give penicillin to sick cows. The sick cows give milk. The milk's full of penicillin. The Milk Marketing Board tests for it. If they find any in the tanker they send it back, won't pay for it. But with new wonder Bio-eater – in goes the milk into the tanker, in goes a spoonful of Bio-eater, and five minutes later – everyone's happy. The cow, the farmer and the MMB.'

Natalie thought a little.

'But mightn't that be bad for the person who drinks the milk?'

'Farmers don't drink milk,' said Bernard, 'that's all I know.'

'If you don't do this job,' said Natalie, 'someone else will.'

'You mean let them get nerve poisoning,' said Bernard, 'not me. Take a look. Are my hands trembling?'

He held them out for her inspection, and they were indeed trembling. She took them in her own to steady them. 'Just nerves,' she said, and then rather hastily let his hands go. If it hadn't been for Flora, if it hadn't been for Angus, both reckoned they'd have gone off in the bushes together sooner or later, but neither said anything to the other about that. The sun shone, birds sang (a few), farmers came and went, and paid Bernard over the odds for his trouble, heaving the dusty sacks as he did onto their trucks, and he put off handing in his notice for another week, and Natalie sang as she hammered. That's what a little response from the other sex will do. Or from the same sex, come to that.

Arthur came up to look at the float, but looked at Natalie instead.

'So, how are you doing?' he asked. 'You're looking just fine. Why don't you come by and see me some time?'

'Angus wouldn't like it,' said Natalie.

'Angus doesn't own you,' said Arthur.

'Yes he does,' said Natalie, firmly.

'He's married,' said Arthur.

'So are you,' said Natalie.

'That's different,' said Arthur. 'My wife doesn't understand me.'

And he laughed, and she laughed, politely. Arthur went away and told Angus that Natalie would never have the float ready in time: she'd need reinforcements. He'd felt obliged to try his luck, so charming had Natalie looked, in her white, painters' overalls, her role changed once again, no longer a deceitful wife but taken a step or so back into little-girl dependency, so that she seemed altogether new and fresh. Just as well, of course, not to tread on Angus' toes, but life got boring, and Sandra was becoming too serious, and had taken to calling Jane at home and putting down the receiver when she answered. Natalie would never have done a thing like that.

Angus went zooming up in the Quattro to inspect the float and was concerned by its state of unreadiness.

'Don't worry,' said Natalie. 'It'll be all right on the night.' But he knew it wouldn't be.

The float was ninety feet long. At one end, fifteen feet high and roughly hewn out of balsawood, but not yet painted, was the image of a kindly estate agent. He held a giant key in an outstretched hand, which would slowly rise and fall as the float moved. Over the other end loomed a noble auctioneer, whose hammer would similarly rise and fall, as its owner turned his smiling head from side to side. Standing firm enough along the edges of the float were ranged the frontages of ideal homes, but not yet completed with the expected lace curtains and pot plants. Standing behind each house was to be an ideal housewife (circa 1955) in frilly apron waving a feather duster (not yet acquired) with a happy smile. They were not yet organized. A thousand light-bulbs, not yet strung, were to burn overhead: music, not yet selected, would come from the loudspeakers. 'Our House' (Madness) was Natalie's favourite, but had a satirical edge that worried WAEADA, so no decision had been made. 'I'm Dreaming of a White Christmas' (Crosby) was another possibility with 'Old-Fashioned Girl' (Kitt) coming up fast on the outside. The theme of the float was to present WAEADA as an altruistic body whose only concern was good housing and happy marriages untroubled by serious debt. 'WAEADA – the Housewife's Friend' was yet to be emblazoned along the side of the edifice. But the conch throne was elegantly and beautifully finished in silky white. Fluted swan's wings curved up and over it. 'Isn't it lovely!' sighed Natalie, and how could Angus be cross? He kissed the back of her neck and went off with her into the paint shop behind the barn. Bernard gritted his teeth and sold another packet of New Wonder Bio-Eater without a single twinge of conscience. 'We'll have to get you helpers,' said Angus to Natalie.

Arthur had offered Flora the role of Mrs Housewife Princess: she who was to sit on the throne. She'd come up to the shop one day with rather a nice painting she'd found on the skip outside her front door, up at the rubbish tip.

'Who, me?' she said. 'A housewife? You must be joking. What am I housewife to? A caravan?'

'We're not fussy,' said Arthur. 'No one will mind. You're liked round here.'

'I'm not even married,' said Flora.

'Who is, these days?' he asked.

'You, for one!' she said. 'Anyway,' she added, 'me sit on a white throne? You have to be a virgin to do that, and I'm no virgin.'

Her instinct was right. Only virgins should sit on white thrones, and even then it's tricky. In the early days of the carnival they'd like as not burn their chosen virgin to death. At first on purpose – later on by accident on purpose. That was the point of the event. Burn a virgin, fire a barn, drown a witch. Clear old scores and start afresh! What do you think the carnival is about? Fun and games? Oh, no.

'We can do without a virgin,' said Arthur, taking her pretty white hand. 'We can't do without you!'

'You give me back my hand,' said Flora. She was looking particularly pretty that day. She had gold sparkle in her hair and silver dust on her smooth cheeks, and wore one of Bernard's leather jackets over a shabby suede miniskirt, and high, though broken, stiletto heels. He feared for his floor.

'You just give me a proper price for my painting,' she said. 'That's all you're here to do. You leave all that other to younger, sillier folk than you.'

He did not take offence. He liked Flora. He looked a second time at the canvas – maple framed, thick with grime but with quite a nice flower painting lurking beneath, and saw that it was better than he'd at first assumed. He thought it might even be worth putting into auction. He offered her a tenner.

'Bernard says,' observed Flora, 'that if you get offered a tenner it's probably worth five hundred. If you get offered between two and five, then it's worth about twenty.'

'Bernard doesn't know what he's talking about,' said Arthur, but Bernard did. The more you offered, that was the trouble, the more the public thought you were cheating them, and the more likely you were to be doing just that.

'A tenner,' he repeated, 'and I'm doing you a favour.'

'It's a really nice picture,' she said. 'I know it is, and if there was room in the caravan I'd hang it up.' He believed she would, and it endeared her to him, even more than her long slightly bowed legs and her wide eyes and her glitter-dusted brows. If only Jane had appreciated antiques, liked beautiful things, how happy they might have been!

'Tell you what,' he said. 'I'll put it in auction, I'll take 10 per cent dealer's fee, and you be Mrs Housewife Princess.'

'It's a deal,' she said. She didn't believe the bit about only 10 per cent – 90 per cent would be more like it, and how could she ever check – but she was hungry.

'If you want a job,' he added, 'go on up to Avon Farmers and help them out on the float. One pound the hour.' She went. Arthur thought she was wasted on Bernard; he always had.

And that's how it happened that Natalie, Sonia, Flora, Ros, and presently Arthur's Jane were all up at Avon Farmers working on the float in the first week of November just to get it ready. The weather was closing in. The barn was draughty, wind swept the rain across the fields outside in visible sheets, but inside there was warmth and camaraderie, 90p the hour and no questions asked and so what if Flora was getting a pound. Sonia's and Ros' children warm in school, with the State paying the heating bills. Something to *do*. There were no complaints, not at first.

Praxis

But Sonia wouldn't let things go along happily, would she! Sonia wanted justice. Sonia wanted to get to the root of things. Sonia bore a grudge. Sonia knew the history of the carnival – all those afternoons with Edwina, hanging about, out of the cold in the Folk Museum, had not been wasted. Sonia wanted her past to catch up with her present. Sonia hated men. Sonia hated men in the same way as Angus and Arthur, Harry, Stephen and Alec, to name but a few, hated women. It's just that men have power and women don't, so men smile and kiss women and hardly know they hate them, even while they hurt them, and women like Sonia, who hop around the world with as many limbs tied as they have children, turn shrill and desperate and go mad so the men can see them coming and get out in time. Maenads, harridans, hags, witches – don't look at the Medusa, sir, or you'll see yourself in her mirror eyes, get turned to stone! Harpy hair and writhing snakes! Shall I tear out a snatch of my hair and hand it to you? Would you like that? No?

A pill, please. I must finish the story.

The WAEADA float was to take to the road on the Wednesday night. On the Tuesday morning Arthur's wife Jane came up to see if she could help. She was carrying the leather bucket. Her cheeks were hollow and her eyes were red with crying, but her clothes were expensive. The others were dressed by Oxfam.

'Are you sure you want to?' asked Sonia. 'We're all on the dole. You don't want to get infected.'

But Jane said Arthur had sent her up. She cried into her pot of paint until finally Ros asked her what was up. She said that she kept getting telephone calls from someone who put the phone down when she answered and it was getting her down. 'You mean it might be one of Arthur's fancy women?' asked Flora, right out. 'Don't you take any notice of those: those are just his sillinesses. Arthur's all right.'

'She wouldn't keep ringing if it was still going on,' said Ros. 'Whatever it was, it's finished.'

But in spite of this comfort Jane still trembled and wept so much she had to be given a cup of tea.

'Marriage!' she said. 'But what's the alternative? I'm too old to start again. And he can do as he pleases because what in the world is there to stop him?'

'You *can't* stop them,' said Natalie, 'all you can do is feel differently about it in your head. You can learn not to care.'

What did Natalie know about it? What she'd lost to Marion Hopfoot was nothing. What Jane was losing was really quite something. What Sonia had lost was even more. Natalie saying what she did made Sonia even crosser. While women adapt, and adapt and adapt, men will continue to get away with everything. If Jane hadn't come up weeping and wailing to the barn at Avon Farmers, if Natalie hadn't been so complacent, perhaps what was to happen wouldn't have happened.

'I reckon,' said Sonia, laying down her paintbrush, 'you *can* stop men doing things.'

'How?' asked Natalie. These days her attitude towards Sonia was not quite antagonistic, but certainly somehow defiant.

'For one thing,' said Sonia, 'you can stop colluding.'

Ros was busy lettering in the 'F' of Housewife's Friend. She laid down her brush.

'They're not really our friends, are they!' she said. 'Why should I paint lies?'

'Because they pay us to,' said Flora, but she put down her hammer. She'd been tacking Terylene lace around the toy town windows. And Natalie, who had been stitching Velcro onto the estate agent's waistcoat, stopped that as well. Jane snivelled on for a time, but presently was quiet. It was she who spoke first.

'I suppose,' she said, 'that giant at the back is really Angus, and that one in the front is Arthur. So why don't we make them look like who they really are?'

And Sonia hardly had to say a word. Of their own accord, out of their own oppression, they were back in the ancient spirit of carnival, when the images of the hated were paraded through the streets, and hung from gibbets, or rolled down the hills in burning tar barrels.

They worked through the evening and into the night, and one of those wonderful late autumn evenings it was, when the sun struck low from behind the Tor, and the red lingered in streaks across the sky, and fog formed in puffy lines low over the levels, and reflected the red upward. Oh yes, a numinous evening indeed. Around carnival time, such evenings are common.

Early the next morning Angus and Arthur came up to have a last look at the float. It was covered by a tarpaulin.

Natalie distracted Angus, and Flora distracted Arthur, and each assumed the other had looked beneath. The float was to travel to Glastonbury pulled by Bernard on the tractor, with a generator for the lights tagged along behind. The girls, together with Angus' Jean, Pauline from the delicatessen and Sally Bains from the school office as reinforcements, were to change into their housewife costumes in the carnival headquarters. The WAEADA float was no. 62; no. 61, travelling ahead, was to be a ninety foot monster – 'Baghdad Nights' and no. 63, behind, was to be a 'Star Wars' spectacular. Bernard would steer the float to its place in the appropriate layby, and when evening came, the tarpaulin would be rolled back, its merry band of housewives would ascend, Flora, dressed in virgin white, would take her place on the pale swan throne, the generator would hum, the myriad overhead lights would blaze, music would blare and no. 62 would move off.

Human Sacrifice

All these things came to pass.

Arthur and Angus caught up with the float as it rounded the War Memorial corner. Here the crowds were thick and uncomfortable, those behind moving forward to see the better, those in front stepping back so as not to get their feet run over. Brilliant light interwove with patches of darkness: near music mingled with far, blowing in the wind. Marshals attempted to keep the front ranks back, in vain. Children kept breaking from the crowd to buy the silvery balloons, or the horrid hot dogs, or just to play chicken in between the massive, slowly moving structures. The heady smell of hot diesel oil was all around. The procession would stop from time to time to allow its back to catch up with its front, or when a tractor broke down, or some wider than allowed float failed to manoeuvre a corner and had to be manually backed to start the attempt again. Few floats could go into reverse gear. On the WAEADA float Natalie, Sonia, Ros, Jane, Jean, Pauline and Sally gazed enigmatically out on the crowds, and smiled, and waved their feather dusters.

The music that blared out from no. 62 was not 'Our House' or even 'Fly me to the Stars' but Pete Seger's all too recognizable 'Little Boxes':

> 'Little boxes, on the hillside,
> Little boxes, made of ticky-tacky – '

And the auctioneer, of course, was an all too recognizable version of Angus, with fair floppy hair dropping over a self-indulgent brow and a double chin, raising and lowering his hammer. And there was Arthur at the other end of the float, with his yellow waistcoat and his spyglass in his cunning eye, and the key to his back room offered, taken away, offered, taken away – no, as portraits they were not kind.

Some of the crowd sniggered as the familiar pair soared by above them, but on the whole most assumed that what they saw was meant, intended, by persons who knew better than they. They clapped and applauded, and only a child was heard to say, 'But that man isn't smiling, he's snarling like my dog.' And if only those on the float got the full significance of the blow-up of Ros' last postal draft plastered over the back of the float, never mind. A full eighteen pounds and sixty-one pence! Landlords live by the DHSS here in the heart of the country. Many, in fact, will take only tenants in receipt of public funds. Rent gets paid direct, and never fails.

'Bitch!' shouted Angus to Natalie, keeping pace with the float. 'What have you done?' She looked away, smirking, it seemed to him. 'Ungrateful bitch!' But a surge of the crowds came between them, and the music rose all around to deafen him and she seemed to forget he was there altogether. Arthur, on the contrary, seemed to see the joke. He laughed and puffed as he walked beside the float, parting the crowds. He called out to Flora, 'I've got something for you!' but she was too busy being Mrs Housewife Princess of Ticky-Tacky Land to hear.

'Bitch!' cried Angus to Natalie, catching up again. He was beside himself at her treachery. He had given her everything and now look, she had been laughing at him all the time.

'You never loved me,' she shrieked down at him above Pete Seger and the crackle of lights and the hum of generators and the cries of street sellers. 'You only wanted me because Arthur wanted me.'

'I don't love you!' he shouted, above the roar of the tractors and the yells of children – 'not after all this. Bitch!' Oh, he was over excited!

'I thought for a week I loved you,' said Natalie, 'because I needed you and there was no one else, and you have to have someone. But I don't love you any more!'

'Thank God for that,' he shrieked. 'I want you out of that flat by the end of the week.'

'Don't worry,' she yelled. 'I will be!'

And she waved her feather duster at him and brushed him out of her life.

Angus ran ahead to tell Bernard, who was driving the tractor which pulled the float, that he was fired, but Bernard was chanting a little song, in his fine West Country burr. It went like this:

'Dieldran, mecadox, antimicrobae
Auteomycin, chlorotetraclin,
Magic sulphameyathhe, and wonder Bio-eater – '

'You're fired!' shouted Angus again. It was hardly fair of Bernard. All these substances were being phased out up at Avon Farmers in favour of those which had EEC approval.

'I fired myself yesterday,' said Bernard. 'I'm pulling this float for the love of it. I went to a funeral yesterday. My mate the gravedigger told me human bodies took a long time to decompose these days, they're so full of preservatives. You keep your wage packet. I'd rather sell smack at the school gates any day. It's safer.'

'Little boxes, on the hillside . . .
And they're all made out of ticky-tacky . . .'

sang Pete Seger, as he's been singing since the fifties.
Nothing changes.

I said my piece then, from my moving stage. I
shouted it at the crowds. Most of them didn't hear. If
they did, they thought I was part of the act.

I told them about the wickedness of men, and the
wretchedness of women. I told them they were being
had, cheated, conned. That they were the poor and the
helpless, and the robber barons were all around. They
were being poisoned for profit: their children were
being robbed of their birthright: the very rain that fell,
the forests that grew, were being sold off, to be resold
back to them. That they lived here in the heart of the
country in the shadow of cruise missiles, in the breeze
from Hinkley Point. That it was up to the women to
fight back, because the men had lost their nerve. The
crowd applauded my performance, though they missed
the gist of the words. That was something. I pointed
to the effigy of Angus on my right and Arthur to the
left.

'I blame the guilty men,' I yelled. 'Seducers, forni-
cators, robbers, cheats!'

How they cheered!

And this was the signal for my friend Ros to pick up
the Georgian leather bucket, standing so innocently
there beside Flora's conch throne, but actually filled
with petrol by me just before I began my speech. Ros
flung the contents over Angus' effigy. I flung a lighted
match after it. I hadn't realized quite what the impact
of flame on petrol is. In a word, startling. The crowd
yelled, in horror, surprise and, I fear, delight.

Fire's wonderful. So pretty, don't you think? Not

final and grudging and finite, like an explosion, but always offering a tentative, if noisy, way out. If, if! cries the fire. If I don't catch, shrieks fire. If you've got water, if you can block out my oxygen, find the blanket and locate the extinguisher, perhaps, just perhaps, I'll let you off this time! I'll go out. Any offers? Got any ifs for me? What? None? And then stronger and stronger comes the roar – no, no stopping me now, no putting me out; on your head be it. See, I'm unquenchable, I'm everywhere, everything, crackle, leap and bound and lo – all gone! Up in flames, into ashes, into dust, goodbye!

It took the housewives on the float a moment or so before they realized what had happened. Fire has that effect. You tend to stare at rapidly ascending tongues of flame, and admire their beauty, before realizing they can hurt, burn and destroy. They leapt from the float in what I see as the order of their desire for survival. Jean was off first (she would!) then Natalie, then Ros, then Sally, then Jane, then Pauline and then myself, Sonia. I would quite happily have died there.

And Flora?

Flora didn't get off the float at all. She was mesmerized not by the flames but by her good fortune. What had happened was that Arthur had just handed her a cheque for two thousand pounds. He'd put her flower painting into a Sotheby's sale and it had fetched two thousand two hundred. He'd taken for himself only 10 per cent and he need never have mentioned the sale at all. He'd done what he said he would. He had achieved a moral act, finally. It killed Flora.

People shouldn't change their natures, just like that. It doesn't do. Surprise is bad for people. It was sheer surprise which kept Flora sitting there gawping at the cheque. The light bulbs on the top of the float were cracking and popping in the heat. The crowd was now bending backwards and away out of danger. There were shouts and cries: Bernard was uncoupling the tractor. 'Baghdad Nights' was standing off: 'Star Wars' was being manoeuvred backwards.

Flora sat all in virgin white on the voluminous snowy throne and no one noticed her in time, just sitting there. I think it was her very stillness made her invisible, her very whiteness. Oh my virgin sacrifice! Allow me to descend into maudlin sentiment, just for once. She was all of us, what we once were, young, pretty, innocent and stunned by the wonder of the world, its capacity suddenly to offer good when all that is expected is bad. The giant effigy of Angus toppled back towards the centre of the float, and loomed over the throne, as some kind of root fixture burned through, and bent back still further, and cracked, and down it fell on top of the throne, on top of Flora, and Flora died. I think from the smoke. I hope from the smoke. Something horrible in the foam upholstery. I don't think she *burned*.

Okay. She burned. Consider it. A paragraph of silence while we do. Memorial space, dedicated to writhing, horrified, twisting Flora. My fault.

And to the others we all know, who died horribly before their time. Not my fault.

My fault? Ros threw the petrol, I threw the match. I could make Ros do anything I wanted, and I did. Only Ros and me knew what we were going to do. Our demonstration. Our visual fix, so the crowds would know the way the heart of the country was going, and do something about it. So it landed me here. Fine! Flora, the virgin sacrifice, so the world could cure itself of evil and renew itself? Better still! I hope it works. I didn't mean Flora to die, or anyone to die, of course I didn't. Fate took a hand. I take it as a good omen that it did. Bad for Flora, good for mankind, in which of course we include women, the lesser inside the greater.

My guilt, my madness if you like, has been the murder in my heart. I don't deny it; how can I? Because of the misfortunes of my life I have been murderous, full of hate. The fire didn't put those feelings out: on the contrary, it inflamed them, at least for a while. Eddon Hill drugs, Dr Mempton's patience, something, has worked. I feel quite denuded of hate, all of a sudden, as if Flora had stepped down, all virgin white, and graciously extended her lily white hands, that she never once got in the scrubbing bucket, no matter how Natalie Harris and Jane Wandle nagged, and forgiven me. Well, and why not! I was only trying to help.

Resolutions

Flora had a funeral to which everyone came. Ros got probation; I got put in here. Something happened to Arthur, who put on weight and aged ten years between the carnival and the funeral, and lost the knack of pulling women. Or so Ros told me. He tried Ros and she simply laughed. Perhaps his good deed did him no good: made his Dorian Gray picture in the attic grow younger so he had to grow older. Virtue is its own reward, don't think it isn't, and sometimes it's a positive drawback. Anyway, with Arthur less randy Jane was happier. Only when she has him helpless in a wheelchair, after a stroke, will she be truly at ease. Sometimes I understand why it is that some men fear some women so: if women are virtuous, if they insist on being victims, then their misery controls to the grave.

Angus? Angus did not forgive Natalie. He was tired of her, anyway. He'd said she could have the flat free until November, just about getting the timing right. He did not renew the lease, but when he'd calmed down did not deny she'd brought richness and happiness into his life, at least for a while. Jean was rather pleasanter to him, now she was on HRT, or hormone replacement therapy. Her horribleness turned out to be menopausal. Or so he said. Various West Country rings dealing with illicitly imported agricultural chemicals, were uncovered by the police, and the penalties weren't just fines but prison sentences, so Avon Farmers disappeared only just in time. Arthur started a Garden Centre there instead, where the flowers and shrubs flourished immoderately, and where not a butterfly ever alighted. Something had indeed got into the soil, for good or bad. One of his assistants had a baby born with a crooked leg but that could happen to anyone: there's an epidemic, remember, of handicapped babies. And another died of cancer, but that was hardly statistically surprising, and in the meantime, how the pot plants in Eddon Gurney bloomed!

In the delicatessen the till pinged almost nonstop and profits grew, against all expectation. With the coming of Jax had come good fortune. The animal was obviously happier in a home where there were no children. Gerard took anti-depressants and lost his social conscience and thereafter sold luxury foods to the non-hungry with equanimity. Pauline took up weight training: an excellent substitute for sexual activity for those whose husbands grow elderly and uninterested too soon for their liking.

Val Bains' back got permanently better at carnival time. He was in the crowds watching when float no. 62 caught fire. He ran forward to help Bernard unhitch the tractor, and in bending and forgetting released some trapped nerve or other in his spine. He took the job in Street at a firm using the new computer technology; it was exacting work if not well paid. He would drop Sally off at work, and collect her on the way home. She was pleased to have so visible and caring a husband.

Natalie? Well, here's a turn-up for the books. Natalie stepped into Flora's shoes, with Bernard in the caravan, up by the tip. He's ten years younger than she is, but who cares? She had nowhere to go when Angus turned her out of the flat, and she's always got on well with Bernard and at least didn't have the children to worry about. Ros went up to see her, not long ago. Natalie said she was happier than she had ever been in all her life. She was properly alive at last, she said, though looking forward to the spring. Winters in a caravan can be trying. No, she didn't want the children back. What could she offer them? Ros thought perhaps she was on drugs. It was so damp and muddy up by the tip, and Natalie looked so happy without any real reason that Ros could see. But perhaps it's just sex, sex, sex; you know what Bernard is, forever quenching his moral and mental torment in fleshly pleasures. I hope it is. God knows what will happen to her next: what does happen to the one in three women with children whose marriages end in divorce?

You are right, it's worrying about that which has driven me into the nuthouse, and right out the other side. I am, alas, sane again. I am, Dr Mempton says, fit to leave. Why is he being so nice to me? What? I can hardly believe him. How many sessions with the psychiatrist does an ordinary patient have? he asks. One a week? One a *fortnight?* He's joking. That is a monstrously low figure. Yes, I do realize he's been coming *every day*. It did seem strange. I now see it's bloody irresponsible, if what he's saying is true.

Love? Me? Who could love me? I make him laugh, Bill Mempton says. When was making someone laugh a recipe for love? This is very, very embarrassing, and not what I had in mind at all. Look at me! Puffy face, puffy hands, twitching. That's the drugs. I talk too much. I am full of hate and self-pity. He knows that, better than anyone. He'll be saying next all I need is the love of a good man. My God, he's said it! Do Them Upstairs go for this sort of thing -- doctor-patient romances? I hardly think so! Or is it that they reckon anything is better than the Eddon Method? Those deaths must have shaken management no end!

The Heart of the Country

Not for Sonia Flora's triumphant puff of smoke, her exaltation: not for Sonia Natalie's glorious debasement: no, for Sonia comes a proposal of marriage from a good man, who knows her every failing. She can't accept, of course. Happy endings are not so easy. No. She must get on with changing the world, rescuing the country. There is no time left for frivolity.

Fay Weldon
Mid October 1986